KU-152-768

NEBULA

Physicist Lance Barley couldn't explain the presence of a half naked woman in his laboratory. The consequences would be serious for him. He knew the laboratory had been securely locked. It was impossible for anyone to have entered — and the place was empty before he started up the generators in the Transmutation Laboratory. However, following completion of his experiment, the lights had come on — and there she was! An exquisitely beautiful girl — but she was also a deadly murderess!

Neath Port Talbot Libraries	
CL	
Date	PR
LOC	
No.	

JOHN RUSSELL FEARN

NEBULA

Complete and Unabridged

LINFORD
Leicester

First published in Great Britain

First Linford Edition
published 2009

Copyright © 1950 by John Russell Fearn
Copyright © 2009 by Philip Harbottle
All rights reserved

British Library CIP Data

Fearn, John Russell, *1908 – 1960.*
  Nebula. - - (Linford mystery library)
  1. Physicists- -Fiction. 2. Women murderers
  - -Fiction. 3. Suspense fiction.
  4. Large type books.
  I. Title II. Series
  823.9'12–dc22

  ISBN 978–1–84782–909–2

Published by
F. A. Thorpe (Publishing)
Anstey, Leicestershire

Set by Words & Graphics Ltd.
Anstey, Leicestershire
Printed and bound in Great Britain by
T. J. International Ltd., Padstow, Cornwall

This book is printed on acid-free paper

1

Mystery girl

In the great physical laboratory of Transmutations Limited twenty million volts of man-made lightning writhed and crackled between anode and cathode spheres as base elements were changed into commercial products.

Lance Barclay, the young scientist in charge of the huge and terrifying globes, took his control of millions of volts with complete indifference. For five years now he had spent practically every working day in his small operations-box — an affair like that of a sentry-box, its walls transparent but insulated against dangerous radiations. Upon a massive switchboard were all the dials, panels, and switches necessary for handling the apparatus.

Transmutations Limited, a government-controlled combine which had sprung into being following the development of atomic

1

by-products, existed solely for the purpose of changing base products into more useful substances. The atom-smashing apparatus either added or reduced the number of electrons in any atomic set-up and thereby produced a complete change of state. Lead, for instance, could be converted into cheap commercial diamonds; and zinc could be turned into gold. The dream of the ancient alchemist had come true, but the place was as guarded as the Royal Mint. No possible chance was afforded for a power-hungry scientist to change metals into gold for his own use — or misuse.

Lance yawned slightly as he watched the fearsome energy coils flashing between the mighty globes. The laboratory was lighted by intermittent glares and grotesque shadows. His particular task at the moment was to transmute three-hundred tons of crude pig-iron into beryllium, urgently needed on an overseas construction job. In a matter of minutes the required metal, now lying in the vacuum tube connected to the globes, would have changed its state.

Outside the laboratory the warning light was at red. Inside it the lightning flickered with more intensity as the seconds passed. Green, blue, lavender, violet, flashing down the massive earthing columns into the floor. As the electrical fury increased it discharged its enormous load into the giant vacuum tube. Slowly the laboratory seemed to quiver as streamers and fireballs of twenty million volts crashed between the globes.

On the indicator in the control-box a pointer came to zero. Lance watched it intently, then closed a switch. The silence seemed uncanny after the hellish fury of the man-made thunderstorm. The dynamos whined to a standstill, as the crepitation of the streamers ceased. Tubes and displays died into black glass . . .

Lance pushed back his damp black hair and mopped his face. There was always a certain emotional strain to his job of controlling the lightning. One slip and he might bring about his own death and destroy the huge building completely. He stood up, not quite six-feet tall and stoop-shouldered, then prowled outside into the laboratory area and switched on the lights.

A door opened. Jeffrey Walcott, a physicist of the higher grade and exclusively engaged on intra-atomics, came in from the outer research annex. He was a heavy-built, thick-set fellow of thirty-two, one tuft of sandy hair nearly always falling across his humorous blue eyes. He had none of the seriousness of Lance with his lean, sallow face and faraway grey eyes — nor had he anything of his brilliance.

'Finished blowing the place up?' Jeff asked.

'Uh-huh.' Lance smiled faintly. 'Same old routine. One thing into another. Makes you think sometimes. Wealth untold under my hands, just by the push of a button, and I remain at a fixed yearly salary as the bonehead in charge of all this junk.'

Jeff grinned. 'Don't go getting ideas, Lance. In any case, I can't see what more you need. You've a nice home, a wife who adores you, two children, and as much money as a man needs these days. Why think of anything beyond it?'

'I'm not doing. Just remarking . . . What brought you in here, anyway?'

4

'I wanted to ask you about the Belmore transmutation. The old boy is playing hell because he didn't get his block of gold for that building he's christening next week . . . '

'He'll get it. I've this to do first. May as well see if I got the beryllium okay.'

Jeff nodded and watched Lance as he strolled over to the huge vacuum tube. He spun the screws, which allowed the sides to fall apart once the air pressure within the tube had been made to equal that of the air in the laboratory. Lance surveyed the tube's interior and straightened. Then he gave a start and looked again. Jeff, watching him, saw his back grow rigid.

'Anything wrong?' he asked, strolling over.

Lance straightened up and turned. There was a most extraordinary expression on his face — as though he had looked at something utterly beyond comprehension. Jeff frowned, then peered into the vacuum tube. All he saw was a heap of metal, recognisable as beryllium in the crude state. He looked over his shoulder.

'You seen a ghost?' he asked bluntly. 'This stuff is just what you'd expect, isn't it?'

'That — that is, yes. Look further — at the far end of the tube.'

Jeff did so, and then he too started violently. Lying on her back, legs doubled under her body and arms flung wide, was a girl! Jeff jerked back his head and blinked — then he met Lance's uncomprehending eyes.

'It — it couldn't *happen*!' Lance declared at last, getting a grip on himself. 'The temperature in the tube would kill all living organisms.'

'Probably it killed her, too. If so, no blame attaches to you. She shouldn't have hidden herself there . . . We'd better get her out.'

Jeff, too, was calmer now. He leaned into the tube and by reaching to the limit managed to grasp the girl's ankles. To his astonishment they were warm, which instantly disproved the possibility of her being dead. It was such a surprise he released her again and stood up.

'Something mighty queer here,' he

muttered. 'Let's take a closer look at her.'

He moved to the end of the tube, in which end the mystery girl was sprawled, and peered down on her through the curvature of the proofed glass. Lance advanced slowly and looked too. Both men were silent, realising many things they had not realised before.

For one thing the girl was attired in a manner that would have hurtled her into a police station had she appeared on the streets. She seemed only to be wearing a swimsuit of golden colour, and very abbreviated at that. Her exposed skin was deep olive in colour and gleamed as though it had been polished. Every limb was perfectly rounded, the neck was long and graceful, and the face exquisite. Though she was unconscious there was vitality and life in her full mouth, the lips slightly open to reveal even white teeth, oval-shaped face, and perfectly straight nose. Her brows and hair were both black — utter black, the colour of midnight in space.

'Very nice,' Jeff commented finally, and being a bachelor he felt entitled to make the observation. 'Though I never saw a skin like it outside the make-up department of a film studio. Fact remains we'd better get her out.'

He returned to the tube opening, grabbed the girl's ankles again, and pulled hard. Her curvaceous limbs straightened under the strain and her body slid along the tube's floor. Hauling her into his arms — a task that he found by no means distasteful — Jeff finally succeeded in carrying her to the nearest bench. Lance pushed aside the bottles and impedimenta, rolled up a spare overall for a pillow, and then the girl was laid down gently.

'She's breathing okay,' Jeff said, rubbing his head in bewilderment. 'I can see her chest rising and falling.'

'What happens if — or rather when — this has to be explained?' Lance demanded in horror. 'It's against regulations to have anybody except an employee in here. How am I supposed to explain this — this half-naked creature?'

'She's no creature . . . ' Lance was studying her with admiring blue eyes.

'She's quite the most beautiful girl I've ever seen . . . Though I suppose it will be tough to explain away,' he admitted. 'Anyhow, she needs a doctor, or something. Even though she's alive she's uncon . . . '

He stopped. The girl had opened her eyes. Lance looked into them, and so did Jeff. They neither of them could fathom what they saw there. They were eyes without pupils, or else they had huge pupils and no irises. Their colour was deep crimson — red circles that were at once terrifying and yet incredibly fascinating.

'I — I never saw anything like her!' Lance said, and with a conscious effort looked away. He felt curiously sickened. The scarlet orbs had turned him inside out. He had the feeling that he had looked upon something unspeakably evil, yet at the same time irresistibly attractive.

'Yes, the eyes *are* queer,' Jeff admitted, studying them intently. 'They seem to be all one big pupil. The red in them is at the back of the eye and . . . '

'Oh, shut up!' Lance yelled at him

suddenly. 'She's something frighteningly different from any woman we've ever known! Come away from her, man!'

'Why? Because her eyes look queer? Don't be an idiot!'

Lance would probably have said more, but at that moment the mystery girl raised herself on a dimpled elbow and looked about her. She put an olive-tinted hand, slender as a willow, to her forehead and smoothed back the tumbled tresses of space-dark hair.

'Who — who are you?' Jeff asked, and watched her beautiful face undergo changes of expression.

She made a reply in an extremely rapid tongue, but it was a reply without meaning. Her voice, though, was music in its essence. It was the tinkle of silver bells, the sibilance of matchless cadences interwoven. It was — baffling. Beyond the comprehension of the two men in the laboratory. They knew more than ever that they were in the company of a being who looked like a woman and yet who was utterly different from any normal woman.

She went on talking in the same liquid tone, until Jeff held up his hand and shook his head. Evidently she realised she was not being understood for she became quiet and her crimson eyes moved from one man to another. Her brows knitted a little and an expression of profound bewilderment came to her face. She started to look about her. Then she sat up completely, put her dainty feet to the floor, and began to stroll round the laboratory.

Jeff cleared his throat as he watched her lissome curves moving with the grace of a panther. She seemed quite indifferent to the brevity of her costume and was apparently trying to fathom her surroundings.

'This is awful,' Lance groaned. 'Somebody's bound to come in soon to ask about that pig-iron job I've done. She'll be found and then God knows what will happen.'

'She's alien — unspeakably beautiful — from another world perhaps.' Jeff seemed to be half-talking to himself.

'Another world? Don't be an idiot!

How could she be?'

'I'm just theorising. You never saw a girl like her on *this* world, did you?'

'No but . . . I just can't fathom it,' Lance insisted. 'That vacuum tube was empty when I started, save for the pig-iron. I am willing to swear that anywhere. Further, the conditions in that tube were only fit to kill life, not create it. As for her belonging to another world . . .'

Lance lost himself in bottomless speculation. At the moment he could only think of contact with another world being made through the medium of rocket-projectiles, and there certainly had not been any connection with *his* work.

'We can't understand her name,' Jeff said thoughtfully. 'So let's give her one.'

'What, for instance?'

'Nebula. It sounds feminine, and it sort of typifies her mystery, her unformed being, her strangeness.'

Lance nodded slowly, then watched the girl as, entirely without embarrassment, she returned across the laboratory. Every movement of her superb figure was poetry itself.

12

'Nebula,' Lance said, pointing to her meaningfully. 'I'm Lance. *Lance.*' He jabbed Jeff. 'This is Jeff. Jeff. You understand?'

She threw back her head suddenly and laughed with the ripple of bubbling waters.

'Nebula,' she agreed, and the way she said it sounded like the music of the spheres. Then Jeff saw something and jumped in amazement.

'Her eyes!' he gasped. 'Look at them!'

Lance looked. The girl was only a few feet away now — alluring in every possible way. In a passing fashion Lance noticed she was perhaps five-feet-six in height; but her eyes . . . They were the colour of sapphire! Great blue orbs with no trace of pupil, all the crimson gone from them. They looked like gleaming jewels in her perfect features.

'We're seeing things,' Lance gulped. 'Or else perhaps she is switching contact lens on her eyes for a joke.'

The laboratory door opened and all possibilities of a joke ended forthwith. Dr. Masters, curator of the laboratories, came in with impatient strides. He was an eagle

13

of a man with acid features and even more acid temperament. He took six strides forward and then came to a dead stop as he saw the incredibly lovely Nebula watching him, one of her rounded hips thrown out alluringly as she bent a knee slightly.

'This is *it*,' Lance groaned, with a look towards Jeff.

Masters cleared his throat and came forward again, the great sapphire orbs of the girl never leaving his face. She was smiling at him, half in welcome, but the smile died as she noticed the look of black disgust on his face.

'Barclay, what the devil is the meaning of this?' Masters demanded, nearly hooting in amazement. 'I'm waiting for your report on the pig-iron conversion and you're fooling about in here with this — this pin-up girl!'

'I — '

'Quiet! Don't interrupt me! Explain yourself!'

The contradictory statement left Lance with his mouth open, so Jeff cut in.

'Things are not as they seem, Dr. Masters . . . '

'I should hope not! And what are you doing here? I thought your job was to work on intra-atomics in the annex, not waste your time on — on *this*.'

'I came in to get information on the Belmore transmutation, sir . . . then this happened. This girl was stowed away in the vacuum tube there.'

A cold sneer quivered on Masters' thin lips. His pale eyes jumped to the girl — who, it seemed, did not appear to feel the coolness of the laboratory despite her unclad condition — then back to Jeff.

'I imagine, Walcott, that you take me for an idiot!' Masters barked. 'How could any woman hide in a vacuum tube? What woman in her right senses would want to, anyway?'

'I don't know, sir. That's just how it happened.'

'It's a complete mystery, sir,' Lance said, rubbing the back of his head. 'She talks in a foreign language and her eyes are queer. To begin with they were crimson — and now they're blue. As you can see.'

Masters looked back at the girl.

'They're brown,' he said bluntly — and Lance and Jeff both jumped. The incredible thing was that the old boy was right. They *had* become brown, and Nebula was laughing silently, as though to herself.

'What all this is about I don't know,' Masters said at length. 'But you'll certainly need to explain it to the Board of Scientists, Barclay — and so will you, Walcott. I'll have to report it to them and they must take the decisions . . . In the meantime, what about that pig-iron transmutation?'

'Finished, sir,' Lance said dispiritedly. 'There's the beryllium in the vacuum tube. It was during that mutation that Nebula must have arrived in the tube.'

'Nebula? Is that this woman's name? I thought you said her language was foreign.'

'We christened her that, sir, for convenience,' Jeff explained.

'I see. Most unconvincing.' Masters' lips tightened as he thought things out. Then he came to a decision. 'I don't know which of you men is responsible for this woman being here, but I do know she has to be removed, and as discreetly as possible. You had better do that, Barclay.'

'Why me, sir?' Lance was looking anxious.

'Because you have the facilities. If this woman is a foreigner, who got here by mistake, then she must have sanctuary until the Board have decided what must be done. Take her to your home and explain the circumstances to your wife. Obviously, Walcott cannot do anything, with only a bachelor apartment.'

'But — but my wife will wonder what on earth I'm playing at!' Lance objected.

'She will not be alone in that, Barclay. If you didn't want to get into difficulties you shouldn't play such tricks. Get this woman out of here — and lend her an overall. You can consider yourself suspended from duty until the Board has reached its decision. So can you, Walcott.'

Masters did not waste any more time. He strode to the vacuum tube and looked inside it at the beryllium, then glanced over his shoulder.

'Satisfactory enough,' he said briefly.

'I'll have some men in to remove the metal. You'll be notified when the Board has convened a meeting. Never in all my experience as curator of these laboratories have I witnessed such flagrant disregard of the regulations.'

He went on his way and slammed the laboratory door behind him. Lance compressed his lips.

'Fired,' Jeff said, shrugging. 'And none of it our fault. But I can't find it in my heart to blame Nebula. She's far too nice a girl.'

'If that's how you feel about it you'd better come along home with me and lend your support when I try and explain to Elsie. I've a feeling she won't believe me . . .'

'Willingly — as long as I'm with Nebula.'

Jeff hurried across to the locker and brought out an overall. He handed it to the girl and motioned her to don it. She did not seem to understand to commence with, so Jeff was forced to hold it for her whilst she drew it into place. The buttons baffled her completely, so he fastened them whilst he studied her beautiful face. No doubt about it: her eyes had turned brown. They were big, velvety pools watching him intently.

'Jeff?' she asked, in her musical voice, trying to remember.

'I'm Jeff,' he assented, nodding. 'That's Lance, and you are Nebula. Now let's get out of here . . . '

Lance's car whirled them to his home in the London suburbs in a matter of fifteen minutes, and throughout the trip Nebula sat in silence at the back, Jeff on her right-hand side. She watched the traffic and seemed to be pondering it, or else she studied the buildings. If she was putting on an act it was a remarkably clever one. She seemed to be genuinely bewildered by her surroundings. Lance, forced to keep his attention on driving, had no time to study her, or converse with Jeff: in fact his whole attention was occupied in trying to devise a reasonable excuse for Elsie.

Elsie, for her part, was blankly astounded when her husband, Jeff and Nebula walked into the house in the middle of the morning and surprised her in the midst of vacuuming.

'Er — something came up, dear,' Lance said, with an uneasy grin.

'Oh?' Elsie, with all due respect, was not an efficient girl, and certainly she had no claims to genius. She was content to be the wife of a scientist and spend her time looking after home and children. To her, science was the most boring profession in the world.

'This is what came up,' Jeff added, as Lance fumbled for words — and he nodded to Nebula.

Elsie studied Nebula for a moment, then a horrified look crossed her round, fleshy face. She swallowed hard and began to back to the door.

'What — what is she?' she gasped. 'She's — horrible! Look at her eyes! They're all bloodshot, or something.'

Lance looked — so did Jeff. Nebula's eyes were crimson again: those terrifying orbs that seemed to reflect unspeakable evil.

'Her eyes are queer,' Lance said. 'Some kind of ailment. We've got to get that part worked out. Elsie I know how this looks, but this poor girl hasn't a home — and hardly a stitch of clothing under this overall.'

'How do you know?' Elsie asked, disconcertingly.

'Well — er — when she arrived she was in a sort of swimsuit, and she's still wearing it. She's a foreigner, and doesn't understand our customs. You can see she's foreign. Look at the queer olive tint of her skin, and her eyes . . . '

'They're ghastly!' Elsie broke in, staring at them as the girl smiled and waited.

'Only some fault of the iris pigment,' Lance assured her. 'Anyway, I had to bring her here. Jeff couldn't take her since he's a bachelor — so I'm afraid she must stay with us for a while.'

Elsie came forward again slowly, catching at Lance's arm.

'Lance, what in the world are you talking about?' she asked in wonder. 'Do you seriously mean that you are bringing this — this queer-looking woman into our house?'

'Not from choice, dear. Necessity.'

'But — but it's unheard of!'

'So is Nebula,' Jeff said, and explained away the name. Then he told the whole story and finished up by looking very chastened.

'I don't wonder you got discharged. I don't wonder Dr. Masters wouldn't believe you!' Elsie's voice was quivering with fury. 'And now, to add insult to injury, you actually bring this woman into this house! Well I won't stand for it, Lance. I'm your wife, and entitled to protest. Besides, what are the children going to say? Thank heaven they're at school at the moment.'

Lance rubbed his head again and glanced towards Nebula. She was half leaning against the mantel-shelf now, surveying the room as though trying to decide whether she liked it or not.

'I've an idea,' Jeff said abruptly, snapping his fingers. 'If I stay too we can tell everybody she's a friend of mine — as I hope she is. That will take the load off your shoulders, Lance, and make things right with you, eh, Elsie?'

'Well, I don't know . . . ' Elsie made a

bothered movement. 'You're welcome to stay, Jeff, as you often do — but as for Nebula . . . '

'I'll keep her in tow,' Jeff promised. 'In fact, I'll enjoy every minute of it. We shall have to inform the police, of course, She's a missing person and may even have relatives who are looking for her at the moment.' Jeff paused and reflected. 'There's an answer somewhere to all this,' he mused. 'And it is scientific. Otherwise Nebula would have died in that vacuum tube. Our job is to find out who she is, where she came from, and how she got into the tube.'

'In the meantime,' Lance said, 'maybe you can lend her some clothes of yours, Elsie. You're about her size, and she doesn't seem to have any of her own.'

'Never in this world!' Elsie declared flatly. 'It's bad enough to have her foisted on to me without parting with my clothes as well.'

But Elsie was the kind of girl who never held out for long, and in half an hour, the worst of the storm having subsided, she had been talked into realising the

23

necessity for Nebula staying — at least for a while. Except for her queer eyes, which changed colour at intervals, she seemed harmless enough. She drank the tea and ate the sandwiches that were provided, and most of the time she smiled. To Jeff it was an enchanting smile: to Lance, much more inclined to look below the surface, it had a supercilious quality as though Nebula knew a good deal she was not telling — which was more than possible.

Queer or otherwise, however, her advent had to be reported to the police, so towards noon Lance and Jeff left her in Elsie's care and went to the local police station together The sergeant-in-charge was not exactly helpful.

'No olive-skinned women are reported missing on our lists,' he said, with an air of finality. 'Still I can report it to the Central Bureau. What are the particulars?'

'She's aged about twenty-five,' Lance said. 'Her skin is olive-tinted, quite unlike anything I've ever seen anywhere, and her eyes can change colour.'

'Meaning hazel?' the sergeant asked

heavily, pencil poised.

'No — not that. All iris and no pupil — or all pupil and no iris. Hard to tell. And she has a voice like the sweetest of music and a laugh like the ripple of fairy bells.'

The sergeant breathed through his nose and his eyes had become very round. Then, looking obviously dazed, he wrote down the particulars.

'And if any information comes in concerning her she can be found at my home — 47, Dale Road, Hampstead,' Lance finished.

'Yes, sir. Very good.'

Leaving behind them a mentally clouded guardian of the law Lance and Jeff departed, and as they walked the streets towards home they glanced at each other dubiously.

'All else apart, Lance, we've got to get to the bottom of this business,' Jeff said. 'We've both lost our jobs, and unless we find something mighty convincing to put before the Board when we're hauled over the coals we'll be out of work indefinitely. You know how tough the rules are

. . . We're up against something right outside the ordinary run: that's obvious.'

'And as long as Nebula doesn't understand the language we can get no further,' Lance replied irritably. 'Only thing for it is to try and get her to explain herself as quickly as possible. Even if we work on it day and night.'

Jeff nodded — so full of resolve they both returned to Lance's home. Only Elsie was in the lounge as they entered it, and — most unusual for her — she was reclining on the window seat looking out over the garden. The odd thing was that she was wearing the frock that she had loaned to Nebula.

'Elsie, where's Nebula?' Lance asked her — and to his surprise Elsie's voice answered from the kitchen regions.

'In the lounge, isn't she? That's where I left her.'

Lance glanced back towards the window seat and saw that it *was* Nebula uncoiling gracefully and standing up in her borrowed frock. It was not Elsie at all. Lance pinched finger and thumb into his eyes and gave Jeff a dumb look. Since he motioned helplessly it was plain he had fallen into the same brief error of identity.

'Nebula, we have to teach you the language . . . '

Lance spoke very slowly as he moved towards her in the hope she would understand. She returned him a look that showed her amazing eyes had turned to the greenness of the deepest ocean. So used was he by this time to her inexplicable physical tricks he passed the incident over.

'Language,' he repeated. 'We teach it you.'

'Lang-wage?' And the silver voice broke into an enquiring laugh.

'Words — understand. Information.' Lance looked at her hopefully.

'You sound like a Redskin chief making heap big palaver,' Jeff commented dryly.

'Shut up, will you? This is important.'

Since it was plain the girl had not the remotest idea what was intended Lance motioned for her to resettle on the window seat, then he plumped down beside her and began the barest elements of teaching. He chose simple words and identified them with objects. Jeff settled in a chair and sat watching him, a troubled, rather pitying smile on his face.

Lunch came and went. Teatime arrived and passed. The children came home and were introduced to their foreign 'Aunty Nebula' and were packed off to bed early so they could not ask too many awkward questions. Throughout the period, however, Nebula had evinced an extraordinary willingness to learn and by the time late evening had arrived, to Lance's astonishment, she was able to use short sentences. He could only think that she had some kind of eidetic memory . . .

Elsie, by this time, was as deeply intrigued by the whole business as Lance and Jeff, so whilst they sat on one side of the fire beside Nebula, Elsie sat on the other, sewing — and listening intently.

'Your name?' Lance asked. 'What is it? We call you 'Nebula', I know, but what is your real name?'

'I called Veena,' the girl answered.

'I see. Well, as far as we are concerned you are still 'Nebula'. It suits you better

. . . Now, how did you come to get into that vacuum tube and survive conditions which would have killed any normal person?'

'Veena not die,' the girl shrugged. 'Never die. Eternal.'

'How do you mean — eternal?' Lance asked hazily.

'Come from race that keeps on living.'

Lance gave Jeff a look, so Jeff himself asked a question. 'Where is this race you come from, Nebula? Is it another world, somewhere?'

'Not other world. In space. Race dead — except me.'

'But you just said . . . ' Lance rubbed his head helplessly and blew out his cheeks. 'This is impossible!' he declared. 'It doesn't make sense no matter how we try it. Suppose we try another way . . . How did you get into that tube in the laboratory? That is our problem.'

'Veena — born again,' the girl said, after some thought and this produced a baffled silence.

'She couldn't be,' Elsie said, bodging with her needle. 'That's reincarnation and science doesn't agree that that is possible — or so you say, Lance.'

'It isn't, in the ordinary sense,' he agreed, frowning. 'But this may have a different implication. Born again — which means she lived before.'

'Naturally,' Jeff said.

Lance was silent for a long time, turning over scientific theories in his mind. Most of them fell down under the mental probing he gave them. Yet the predominant point was that the girl was here, alive and well even if enigmatic — so there had to be some scientific law somewhere to explain how she had done it.

'Space — born again . . . ' Lance repeated slowly; then he gave a start. 'I wonder,' he said, musing, 'if it might have anything to do with Eddington's theory of a fortuitous concourse of atoms.'

'Meaning?' Jeff asked, slumped in his chair in thought.

'It's an amazing theory,' Lance answered, brooding, 'but I do believe it's the only one which will hold together. I reason it out this way: Eddington has told us that human beings, and for that matter blades of grass and stars, are nothing else but a fortuitous concourse of atoms, thrown together in such a way that they represent a certain form of matter . . . Suppose something similar has happened in regard to Nebula?'

That began it. Jeff hunched forward in his chair and listened attentively whilst Nebula looked from one to the other. Elsie tried to concentrate for a while, then she found the scientific issues sailing far beyond her and so contented herself with her sewing.

It was midnight when the problem had been thrashed out to the only possible conclusion, but whether it was correct or not Nebula would not — or could not — say. She only smiled, and her eyes had turned as black as her hair.

2

The first murders

The following afternoon the Board of Scientists convened a special session, at which Lance, Jeff and Nebula were ordered to be present. They obeyed, the three of them standing on a raised platform in the centre of a circle. Tier upon tier loomed the faces of the world's greatest scientists in all branches of the profession, and none of the faces looked particularly friendly, either.

The President of the Board opened the proceedings, and made things sound infinitely blacker than they were; then he looked down on the trio from his elevated desk.

'Well, Mr. Barclay, as the prime mover in this extraordinary business, what have you to say?'

'I have the solution, sir, such as it is,' Lance answered.

'Then proceed. We are all attention.'

Lance hesitated, and then plunged. 'I believe, sir — as do Mr. Walcott and this girl herself — that she came amongst us because of the same probability which *could* make a kettle of water freeze on a fire instead of boil.'

'I hope,' the President commented sourly, 'you are not endeavouring to be facetious, Mr. Barclay!'

'I am stating a fact propounded by the late Sir Arthur Eddington,' Lance retorted, nettled. Then from the sheaf of papers he was holding he began to quote: 'In his book *Pathways in Science* he says: 'By a highly improbable, but not *impossible* coincidence, the multimillions of particles making up an organic or inorganic body might accidentally arrange themselves in a distribution with as much organisation as at an earlier instant. The chance of this happening is about one in twenty-seven billion million — which proves that the world, the whole Universe, is a mass of probabilities, drifting towards greater and greater disorganisation and final entropy'.'

33

'Quite so,' the President admitted. 'We know the Law of Probability, entropy, and chance. But are you actually trying to prove that this young woman arrived because of a chance occurrence?'

'Eddingion,' Lance continued, 'approximates the time for the reformation of a former mass of atomic aggregates into a prior set-up at something like three million years. That is purely an arbitrary period, of course: it could be longer or shorter. What I believe is this: This girl has existed somewhere before, and perhaps she died. Her atomic make-up was automatically dispersed, maybe drifting free in the cosmos — *but*, by the Law of Chance, operating in a way which will yet take us centuries to fathom, the exact aggregates to the last detail formed *again* into the identical pattern of a previous time. This fact, and the terrific electrical interplay in the laboratory — where those atoms must have been drifting unresolved at that moment — brought about a sudden reconstitution . . .

'This girl took on a former pattern, even to every detail of her — er

— clothes. So, she lived again. It might never occur again through all time — but on this occasion it *did* happen! One chance in multimillions came off! You must admit, gentlemen, that you might take a pack of cards, shuffle it completely, and yet find it back in the original order when you examined it. That would be a multimillion to one chance, but it *could* happen. And in the case of this girl, it did!'

For a long time there was silence, the scientists murmuring among themselves, then the President spoke again.

'Naturally, Mr. Barclay, we admit the theory of chance, because we are scientists, but how do you account for the *mind* of this girl? If she once died, how does it come about that her mind is operating again?'

'I can only suggest,' Lance answered, 'that a mind is disembodied unless it operates through a particular configuration of atoms — a body. Just as a radio wave is disembodied and meaningless without a receiver to bring it into reality. No two bodies are the same, hence none but the mind *for* that body can operate through it, just as only one wavelength can come through on a tuner in sympathy with that wavelength. On that principle it would seem that the mind of Nebula operated perfectly through her former body — it became disembodied when her body died — but when the same reassembly appeared again her mind automatically operated through the same setup . . . '

'And that,' the President asked, after a long pause, 'is your explanation?'

'As near as I can work it out, sir, yes.'

'Would this girl understand questions if I put them to her?'

Lance nodded. 'Providing they are simply phrased. She has not yet got complete mastery of the language, though she has made enormous strides; which proves she is highly intelligent.'

'Nebula, how much have you understood of the theory just given to explain your arrival here?' the President asked her.

'All,' the girl answered, her eyes as blue as the sky.

'And is it correct?'

'I do not know. Chance does not operate on — er — known law. It might be right: it might be wrong.'

'We might get at it better if we knew where you come from. Is it some other planet?'

'Perhaps. Long, long ago. I cannot remember.'

'She told me she comes from an eternal race which never dies,' Lance put in. 'But I cannot believe that since she must have been dead in order to be re-created.'

'How do you explain that?' the President asked the girl, and she shrugged her graceful shoulders and did not answer.

In the brief silence one of the physicists in the group rose to his feet.

'I submit, Mr. President, that this whole business is so unsupported by logical evidence that it should not be accepted for a moment. Consider the main fact: A girl in a vacuum tube in which the temperature was several thousand degrees, and in the midst of electronic energies powerful enough to change pig-iron into beryllium. It is an insult to our intelligence for us to be asked to believe that any living body could survive that kind of treatment and emerge unscathed.'

Lance gave an uneasy glance at Jeff. Nebula herself merely smiled — that deep, unfathomable smile which concealed so much she had not revealed.

'If she is eternal, by some inexplicable process or other, electric energy and space cold might not injure her,' Lance suggested hopefully.

'If she is eternal she could not have died in the first place!' the physicist retorted — and so brought the problem back to its starting point.

The scientists again began conferring among themselves. The heads nodded, some shook, and the trio on the dais waited for what would happen next. Finally the President silenced the murmurings with his gavel and then gave his pronouncement.

'I am sorry, Mr. Barclay, but your explanation is not satisfactory,' he said quietly. 'My colleagues and I are faced with the inescapable fact that laboratory rules were broken, and the answer is not convincing. The ruling is that you, and Mr. Walcott, be discharged from your duties, and this young woman must be handed over to the authorities within seven days if by that time she has not succeeded in proving her identity beyond all question . . . The meeting is now closed.'

There was nothing that could be done. The ruling was absolute. Lance gave Jeff a look, and he shrugged in return. So with Nebula between them they went slowly from the enormous conference room and out to Lance's car. Once within it they sat brooding for a moment or two.

'It's the damned unfairness of it that gets me!' Lance declared finally. 'Nebula is condemned out of hand; she does not even get a chance to explain herself. How can she when she hasn't learned the language properly?'

'She might, in seven days,' Jeff replied. 'But even if she does, and the explanation is more convincing, she'll be packed off to the authorities and that will be that! You would wonder scientists would be such idiots. Here is a girl who is plainly not like other girls of this world, and they throw up every chance of making contact. I should imagine Nebula can have a lot to tell us when she grasps the language properly . . . Am I right?' he asked, glancing at her.

She smiled enigmatically, her amazing green eyes fixed on Jeff's troubled face. He studied her intently for a while, her fascinating beauty drawing him in spite of himself.

Then, just for a moment, he had that conviction of nameless evil emanating from her and turned to look at Lance.

'There's one way she can be saved from the authorities,' Lance said, thinking. 'I'd do it, but I can't because I'm married . . . You could give Nebula your name. As your wife she would become a citizen and that would end the bother.'

As Jeff said nothing Lance gave him a surprised look.

'What's the matter? From the way you've been talking I'd have thought you'd have jumped at the idea of marrying Nebula.'

'It — it takes thinking about,' Jeff answered, hesitating. 'I wouldn't be just marrying a girl, but an enigma . . . Better drive on to your place, Lance, and let's think it out.'

Lance shrugged and switched on the ignition. In fifteen minutes they were back in the lounge of his home and Elsie had been given the facts. A look of profound discontent and suspicion settled on her face.

'So you are out of a job, Lance, with little hope of getting another as good — and we have Nebula to look after as well! It just can't be done. That's obvious.'

'Jeff has the solution, if he'll take it,' Lance answered.

Jeff hesitated; then Nebula spoke.

'You fear me, Jeff?' she asked softly. 'Why?'

'I don't exactly fear you, Nebula, but I'm not *sure* of you. You're alien — foreign.'

'People marry people of other countries,' she said.

41

'That's different. They're all of the same planet and basic stock. I don't even know where you hail from — and you don't seem able to tell us.'

'I am a woman,' Nebula replied simply. 'What more do you ask?'

Her eyes, deep violet, had taken on that compelling-quality which it was impossible to avoid. Jeff looked into them and could not pull his gaze away; yet all the time he had the inner feeling that here was somebody with the magnetism of a snake. Outwardly beautiful, but inwardly a force for evil more devastating than anything he had ever known.

'I — I think,' he said awkwardly, 'that you should learn the language properly before we marry, Nebula. In that way we can learn something of each other. It's essential.'

'I learn,' Nebula agreed promptly. 'Teach me.'

'During which time you stay here!' Elsie said. 'I might as well tell you I don't like it. I'm not unsociable, but I do feel there's something about you which — '

'Oh, be quiet!' Lance snapped. 'We

have to do the best we can in the circumstances.'

Elsie straightened and said no more, but her bitter expression was proof enough of her feelings ... So Nebula remained, and so did Jeff, and most of the time was spent in teaching her the language. She seemed to have a photographic mind for she could read whole pages of English and then repeat them word for word without effort.

In no way did she encroach on the household, yet her shadow hung over it. Elsie hated the sight of her and made no effort to disguise the fact. The children were wary of her, expressing a child's mistrust in her character. Jeff was perhaps the only one who tried to understand her peculiarities and he flatly refused to agree with Lance that the girl was constantly influencing him against his better judgment.

On the fourth day of language drilling she mysteriously absented herself in the middle of the afternoon. She was nowhere in the house and her bedroom was tidy, but empty. The only one who seemed glad of the news was Elsie.

'Perhaps she's gone!' she said, her eyes bright. 'I can't begin to think how blessed a relief that would be! I'm afraid of her. I have the feeling that she's going to pounce, or kill, or do something terrible at any moment.'

'Ridiculous!' Lance snorted, looking moodily through the window onto the autumn afternoon. 'She's just different, that's all.'

'Sweet enough despite her queer ways,' Jeff agreed. 'I've come to understand her much better these last few days.'

'Well, *I* hope she stops away!' Elsie looked at the clock and then added, 'I'd better fix the tea for the children.'

And at that moment Nebula was standing outside the local school, the collar of her borrowed overcoat turned up about her ears, her hands plunged in her pockets. She removed them and caught at the shoulders of Betty and Jimmy Barclay as they came tripping out of the schoolyard. They looked surprised for a moment.

'Hello, Aunty Nebula!' Jimmy exclaimed

brightly. 'Did mummy ask you to take us home?'

'No,' Nebula answered quietly, speaking perfect English. 'I came of my own accord. I want to talk to you both. Let's do it as we go home, shall we?'

The children had no choice in the matter. With Nebula between them holding each by a hand, they were compelled to run in order to keep up with her lithe, easy strides. Nor did she take the direct route for home; instead she detoured through a park — completely deserted in the grey coldness of the autumn day — and presently turned from its main path and pushed through outcroppings of trees and dense shrubbery.

'Where are we going, Aunty?' asked Betty nervously.

Nebula came to a halt and looked down on the children intently. Her eyes had become crimson again, and all the smile had gone from her full, voluptuous mouth.

'Some day,' she said, 'both of you will grow up. You know that, don't you?'

They nodded dumbly and looked about them for a way of escape.

'When you grow up,' Nebula continued deliberately, 'you will marry. You will have children, who will be like you. I know you are too young to understand that now — but it means you will add new people to the race. And Aunty Nebula doesn't like the idea of that.'

'Why don't you?' Jimmy asked innocently.

'Never mind. Come closer, both of you . . . '

The imperious command in Nebula's voice made the children obey. It was five minutes later when she emerged from the shrubbery. She glanced right and left, smiled to herself, and then returned to the pathway that led to the gates. In ten minutes she was back at the Barclay home.

Lance, Jeff and Elsie looked at her curiously as she came into the lounge. So dull was the day the lights had been switched on and in the artificial glow her weird eyes seemed filled with a myriad dancing fires.

'Where did you go?' Lance asked bluntly.

'I needed air. I am ready now to go on learning.'

'It would be a waste of time,' Jeff told her, and he moved across to put an arm about her shoulders. 'In fact I think you can call yourself 'initiated',' he added, smiling.

She looked from one to the other. 'Then I don't have to go to the authorities?'

'No. That is, if you'll marry me. I've given it a good deal of thought and I've decided to take the risk.'

'Risk?' There was a touch of biting venom in the musical voice.

'Bound to be a risk marrying a girl so strange as you . . . But you can do a lot to explain away the strangeness. Tell us more about yourself. You belong to space, you say. Well, that covers a mighty big area. What else can you tell us? What do you mean by eternal life?'

'I mean — ' Nebula hesitated, then shook her night-black head. 'No, you wouldn't understand. If you want to marry me, Jeff, then I'm willing, but I would have liked a less 'public' proposal.'

'But why? Elsie and Lance here know perfectly well what I intend doing. No sense in hiding it. They'll be the first to congratulate us.'

'Right!' Lance agreed promptly, and came over to shake hands. Not so Elsie: she remained looking at Nebula fixedly, a frown notching her brows.

'You mistrust me, don't you?' Nebula asked her.

'I always have. I always shall. I shall be glad when you have left this house and I hope I shall never see you again.'

Nebula threw back her head and laughed softly, but she did not pass any comment. Elsie glanced at the clock then out onto the darkening evening.

'The children are unusually late,' she muttered. 'I don't understand it — unless they've been kept in for something.'

She left the room in obvious uneasiness and Lance gave Jeff a look as he still held Nebula to him.

'I take it you'll find a fresh job, Jeff?'

'Naturally. I'll manage. Experts on

intra-atomics aren't easy to come by . . . We'll stay one more night, if you don't mind and then tomorrow we'll leave. We can be married at the registry office and after that — Well, we'll work it out. How does that sound, Nebula?'

'If that is what you want, Jeff, then we will do it,' she murmured.

Lance watched them cross over to the chesterfield and settle down side by side, then he mooched out into the hall. Elsie came hurrying to him from the back regions.

'Lance, for heavens' sake see if you can find the children anywhere!' she implored. 'They ought to have been home long ago — and it's getting foggy, too.'

'Right,' he assented, and scrambled into his coat. Elsie watched the front door close and then returned into the kitchen. Under the electric light the table was laid for the children. There was a sound from the hall and Elsie looked round eagerly, then her face relaxed again as she beheld Nebula in the doorway. She was standing so one shoulder rested against the frame. Her peculiar eyes were surveying the room pensively and finally settled on Elsie.

'Something you want?' Elsie asked her briefly.

'I want not just something, but everything,' Nebula replied. 'There are fools in the way who can stop me getting it. Jeff is one of them, Lance is another. You are another. Just as your children were . . . '

'Were?' Elsie repeated, and felt herself grow cold. 'Were?'

'I killed them,' Nebula said, completely casual. 'You see, they would have grown up one day, and by all normal law would have married. There would have been children — more creatures to add to this foul race to which you, your husband, Jeff, and everybody else belongs. To have killed two before they mature may have saved hundreds being born later — '

'What have you done?' Elsie screamed, hurtling forward and seizing Nebula's shoulders. 'What have you done to my babies? *Tell me*!'

Nebula did not answer. She only smiled — but the glow in her awful crimson eyes seemed to glow the brighter. Elsie, who had been conscious many times of the inhuman evil aura that radiated from the woman, recognised it now in all its merciless nakedness. For just an instant she knew what this woman really was — then overwhelming darkness crashed in on her senses and flattened her to the floor.

Nebula looked down at her and then glanced up as Jeff came out of the lounge, attracted by Elsie's shouts.

'What's going on?' he demanded, striding forward. 'What was that Elsie was saying about babies?'

'She had some sort of a fit,' Nebula replied, shrugging. 'Now she seems to have collapsed.'

Jeff looked at Elsie in startled wonder, then went on his knees beside her. His hand went to her pulse and a dazed look slowly came across his face.

'She's — dead,' he whispered.

Nebula's face was expressionless. 'I don't know the meaning of death,' she said slowly. 'I cannot die. I — '

'Don't stand there talking insanely!' Jeff yelled at her. 'Give me a hand to carry her to the settee in the lounge.'

'Why? Don't the dead lie where they have fallen on this world of yours?'

Jeff looked at her bleakly. 'On this world of mine,' he repeated slowly. 'Then you do admit you do not belong on this planet? That you're from — elsewhere?'

'I told you. I came from space. Certainly I don't belong to this retrograde race of which you seem so proud.'

Jeff tightened his lips. Shocks were piling up on him so thickly he couldn't think straight. Back of his mind was a dim wonderment at the fact that he had ever been fascinated by this strange girl with the olive skin and colour-changing eyes. He lifted Elsie's dead weight as well as he could and stumbled with her into the lounge. Nebula followed him up and stood watching. She remained unmoved as Jeff slowly came towards her, his face set hard.

'What did you do to Elsie?' he demanded. 'She was a perfectly healthy woman and certainly hadn't got a bad heart. Her death can only be explained by you.'

'A lot of things can only be explained by me,' Nebula replied, in her most alluring voice. 'And you, who wish to marry me, are the one to whom I shall explain . . . I had nothing to do with her death. You must believe it, Jeff.'

Her arms came up unexpectedly and coiled round the back of his neck. In spite of himself he couldn't resist the soft cling of her body or the lips raised to his. He kissed her and then wondered why he had done it. She held on to him, her very embrace calming his passion.

'Don't think wrongly of me, Jeff,' she murmured, her eyes fascinating pools of violet light. 'Though I may not be of your strange race I love you dearly.'

Jeff gazed into her beautiful face fixedly. Then for some reason he thought of Elsie's poor dead form lying on the floor as he had first seen it — With an abrupt movement he seized hold of Nebula's arms and flung her away from him savagely.

'Don't *touch* me!' he shouted hoarsely, glaring down on her as she lay sprawled on the rug. 'You're poisonous! Just some lovely sort of flower that brings nothing but death and torment. Only you've got a human form . . . But you'll not get me!'

'No?' she asked gently, and her eyes flashed through a bewildering maze of colours until they were flaming scarlet. Queer vibrations battered into Jeff's brain and he tottered helplessly, unable to keep his feet. His legs buckled and he realised he was conscious but unable to move. He lay flat on his back, watching Nebula rise only a short distance away.

'You poor fool,' she said softly; then she turned and left the room. After a moment or two there was the slam of the front door. Jeff lay just as he had fallen, locked in some relentless paralysis from which he could not break free.

It seemed a century before there was a rattling at the front door again, and then the pound of many heavy feet. He found himself seized and lifted into the nearest armchair. He just sprawled as he had been placed, all muscular and nervous control destroyed.

'Jeff, in Heaven's name what happened?' It was Lance's frantic voice shouting at him. 'What's wrong with Elsie?'

'I'm afraid she's dead, sir,' said the voice of a stranger, and Jeff could see now that the newcomers were two constables and a sergeant.

'Dead? *Dead*?' Lance nearly screamed. 'You're telling me that after finding Betty and Jimmy murdered! What in the name of hell has been going on — Jeff, answer me! Damn you, man, say something!'

Jeff found himself punched and pummelled, but it was no use. He could not move so much as his little finger, and certainly he couldn't speak. All he could do was listen.

'Better give me the particulars, sir,' the sergeant said, and to one of the men he added, 'Telephone for an ambulance and a doctor. This gentleman needs attention.'

'Nebula . . . Nebula!' Lance's voice was nearly choked with grief and fury. 'She's back of this! It couldn't be anybody else! Jeff, where is she? For God's sake, man, answer me!'

'I'm afraid he's incapable of that, sir,' the sergeant said, and to the second constable he said, 'Search the house. See if this woman Nebula is anywhere about.'

'Right, sir.'

Before long the sergeant was being informed that nobody else was present anywhere. Lance, his voice dull and dispirited, began describing the girl and by the time he had finished the ambulance had arrived. Jeff found himself hauled into it and from that moment ceased to take any interest in the proceedings. He lapsed into a coma, from which he did not awaken until four days had passed.

But life had come back to him: that was the glorious thing. He was no longer a living brain in a useless body. He could feel, and move — and from then on convalescence began and his strength rebuilt. After a further week had gone by Lance was permitted to see him.

In shocked silence Jeff watched the prematurely grey young man coming towards the bedside. His face was white, the lines in it deeply cut. He walked with an obvious stoop.

'Good to see you mending, Jeff,' he

said quietly, pulling up a chair.

Jeff said nothing but his hand-grip was sufficient to show how he felt. Lance sat down. He pushed his hands through his hair and looked morosely before him.

'They got her,' he said at last. 'She comes up for trial in three more days. You're being given time to recover so you can be a witness . . . God, was there ever such a creature in the name of woman!'

'I still don't know what happened,' Jeff said quietly.

'She killed Elsie and the two children.' Lance sighed as he made the statement. 'How she did it isn't clear yet, but it seems she used some kind of vibratory shock which operated through those hellish eyes of hers. It did something to the brains of Elsie and the children. You resisted it somewhat and so only got paralysis — and modern surgery being what it is you were restored, but it took a complicated brain operation to do it . . . Post mortem on Elsie and the children revealed that the conscious areas of their brains had been blasted to cinders, as though by fire. There's never been anything like it before!'

'Which is one reason why it won't be easy to pin guilt on her,' Jeff muttered.

'It'll be pinned, and it'll stick!' Lance retorted venomously. 'Everything else ties up. She's an alien creature, and admits it brazenly. Her fingerprints are on the children's schoolbooks — and since they died the same way as Elsie it is obviously the same killer in each case. She'll be brought to justice, Jeff, and no murderess ever deserved it more.'

'If she has such mastery over matter, by using mental vibration, she may escape. She might even wipe out the judge and jury — or had you thought of that?'

'I've thought of it. The prosecuting counsel has got special permission to have her blindfolded during the proceedings so her eyes cannot do any damage. That's the way she seems to get her effects — but unless her eyes have X-ray gifts, which I doubt, she'll be powerless. They seem to be her Achilles' heel.'

There was silence for a moment. Outside the big window the dreary branches of a plane tree spread starkly against the grey autumn sky.

'Where was she found?' Jeff asked.

'Running wild in the countryside. Picked her up next day. She made no resistance. She signed a statement admitting she committed the crimes. Signed herself 'Nebula'. It's in all the papers. Never been a case like it. Since she openly admits she is not of this world the thing's caught the public fancy . . . I only wish we were in America, so I could see her executed. I'm not a vicious man, but her utter fiendishness in return for all we've done for her is beyond anything. She deserves to die.'

'She said she is eternal.'

'I don't believe it,' Lance answered stubbornly. 'A woman so unspeakably evil just couldn't have eternal life. It is against all natural reason.'

'She's being defended, I suppose?'

'Yes.' Lance's face clouded for a moment. 'Sir Noel Burgess is taking it on. He's one of the best legal brains of today, too. His fee is being paid by the Interplanetary Society. They believe that Nebula should be saved on the grounds that, to her, destruction of life may not be regarded as a crime. Just as we believe certain pests should be exterminated, so she may think that certain human beings should be wiped out. That is the part I don't like. Burgess has a good peg on which to hang his hat. Since Nebula is not an Earth woman the law may operate to her advantage because she may not come under our rules . . . But she won't escape. That's unthinkable.'

'You hope,' Jeff muttered.

'Dammit, man, whose side are you on?' Lance blazed. 'Or don't you realise what she has done?'

'I ought to, considering what I have been through — but I'm also remembering that a woman of Nebula's accomplishments and inhuman nature may make fools of all the majesty of the law. Or maybe you do not realise how deadly a menace she is? We've turned loose on the world something that never existed before — an evil thing in the shape of an incredibly alluring woman. There couldn't be anything more dangerous.'

'She'll be put away — or something,'

Lance said, but his tone had no ring of confidence. When he came to think, if only for a moment, of Nebula's beauty and fascinating voice he appreciated how difficult it might be for strangers to condemn her.

'Whatever happens I'll support you to the end,' Jeff said at last. 'And to think I contemplated marrying her! She'd have killed me almost immediately.'

'Why?' Lance mused. 'Why? That is the riddle. Even the most evil personality has a reason for hatred. What have we ever done to Nebula except show her kindness?'

Jeff did not answer because he could not. There were unplumbed abysses in Nebula, which nobody could fathom.

3

The trial

Jeff was fit enough to attend the trial as a witness, and when called to the stand, after Lance, he gave every detail exactly as events had transpired. In the packed courtroom the President of the Board of Scientists glanced at his colleagues significantly. Since both young men had told the same story again, under oath, and not contradicted themselves, it began to look as though Nebula really had come into being by accident.

Nebula herself stood in the dock with a velvet, bag-like arrangement over the top of her head. It concealed her night-black hair and covered her eyes. The uncovered lower part of her face was immobile, though at times the full, sensual lips smiled to reveal the perfect teeth.

The prosecuting counsel gave all the facts and called his witnesses, including the fingerprint experts; then came Sir Noel Burgess to give his side of the business. In his final address to the jury he revealed how good a case he had built up.

'My learned friend, the prosecuting counsel, has neglected one or two items,' he said, raising a finger for emphasis. 'No witness actually saw my client commit murder, and the medical experts are all agreed that the cause of death in each case was vibration of an electrical nature. It has been suggested that my client issued, through her eyes, some kind of destructive current, which, conducted by the eyes of the victims, produced their deaths by striking at their brains. I say such a theory is preposterous. As my witness from the Electrical Research Centre has already testified, the vibration given forth by a mental wave is so slight that, without amplification, it produces hardly a flicker on a detector. How, then, could this same power blast the brains of one woman and two children and stun a man? No, ladies and gentlemen, do not allow yourselves to be carried away by such absurdity! Look at my client for yourselves and see if you believe such a thing could be possible . . . '

Sir Noel raised his hand in a signal and one of the wardresses lifted the velvet covering from Nebula's head. Instantly there were gasps of surprise — and particularly from Lance and Jeff as they stared fixedly. For Nebula was a blonde of indescribable beauty, and instead of her eyes seeming all one incredible colour they were blue and normal, with a black pupil in the centre.

She stood with queenly dignity looking about her, that faint smile on her supercilious mouth. Sir Noel Burgess took one long look at her, his professional dignity utterly jolted for the moment. The woman he had seen in prison had been the green-skinned, black-haired creature with the unfathomable orbs; but this woman, as alluring as any queen despite her prison garb, was white-skinned nearly to the tint of alabaster, and the gold in her hair was certainly not that produced by bleach or dye.

'I think,' Sir Noel said, coughing in his

bewilderment, 'that I have made my point.'

'M'lud, I protest!' the prosecuting-counsel cried, leaping up. 'This woman is not the prisoner! She is not Nebula!'

'Then who is she?' the judge asked blankly.

'I — I don't know. Something is desperately wrong somewhere. The real Nebula has disappeared.'

'What is the meaning of this?' the judge demanded, looking at the two baffled wardresses. 'Is this the woman who is on trial, or not?'

'We — er — This is the woman we brought from the cell, m'lud,' one of the women answered in perplexity. 'But she was black-haired then, and olive-skinned. I — I just don't understand it.'

'Fingerprints!' the prosecutor shouted. 'I demand a fingerprint test. That can never lie.'

'Sir Henry, I somewhat deplore the fact that you *demand*,' the judge remarked acidly, 'but nevertheless I am inclined to agree with your suggestion. Fingerprint the prisoner,' he instructed, and waited.

The girl submitted passively to her

slender fingers being pressed onto the impression-pad, then the experts went to work to check the prints with those that were known to belong to Nebula. They looked at each other, then up at the judge.

'The fingerprints do not tally, m'lud,' one of them announced. 'Nebula's prints are whorl; these are arch and loop.'

There was a stunned silence. Never had a courtroom become so quiet in the middle of a trial. At last the judge took a deep breath and looked down on the baffled legal men.

'In the course of fifty years in my profession I have never experienced such audacity, such utter contempt of the letter of the law,' he declared. 'Whoever is responsible for the wrong prisoner being in the court will be severely punished. I just cannot believe that neither of you two gentlemen know what has happened.'

Prosecutor and defending counsel glanced at one another helplessly. Then Lance got to his feet, his face harshly set.

'May I be permitted to speak, m'lud?' he enquired.

'Providing what you have to say is relevant to this extraordinary occasion, yes.'

'In my belief,' Lance said, 'this woman *is* Nebula, but she possesses physical and scientific gifts which are denied to normal men and women. I beg of you to remember that she is not of this world, and has admitted the fact, therefore it is logical to assume that she has powers of which we know nothing. I believe that by some process as yet unexplained she can change her appearance at will.'

The judge's eyes opened wider behind his spectacles but he passed no comment.

'And I've good reason for the belief,' Lance added. 'Not very long ago, when my wife and I had given Nebula asylum in our home, I thought on one occasion that I was speaking to my wife — until I discovered my wife was in another room. In only a matter of split seconds Nebula was Nebula again. It was the only example I ever had of her ability to change her appearance at will into an absolute duplicate of somebody else . . . That, I think, is what has happened

67

now. She has deliberately altered her appearance to throw this court into utter confusion. I say she is still Nebula, and should be tried as such, allowance being made for her uncanny gifts.'

'And her eyes?' the judge asked. 'They seem perfectly normal to me.'

'They are — for perhaps the first time.' Lance made an impassioned movement. 'Judge Hartley, I ask you in the name of the people of this planet to try this woman and have her removed from society. She's the most deadly creature who ever came amongst us. I'm a scientist. I've lived with her. I know what I'm talking about.'

'In that I think Mr. Barclay is right,' said a voice in the audience, and to Lance's satisfaction he saw that it was the President of the Board of Scientists who had risen. 'I was compelled recently to discharge Mr. Barclay and Mr. Walcott from our organisation for what seemed an infraction of the regulations. What has happened since has caused me — and my colleagues — to revise our opinion. This woman is *not* a woman in the ordinary sense, m'lud . . . '

The judge reflected for a moment, glanced towards Nebula's ivory-skinned face and smiling lips, and then back to the tense courtroom.

'I have no other course than to order this woman's release,' he said quietly. 'Whatever your or my personal convictions may be in regard to her, I am only here to dispense the law, laid down in a rigid fashion. It is quite impossible for me to have this woman tried when in every particular, even to fingerprints, she is at variance with the prisoner . . . Case dismissed,' he finished, and tightened his lips.

It looked in the next few seconds as though an explosion had hit the court-room. Reporters blundered over one another to get to the doors; everybody seemed to be talking to everybody else; and Nebula remained surveying the proceedings until the wardresses tapped her on the shoulders and motioned her to return into the back regions to collect her belongings.

'The fools! The blind idiots!' Lance

raved, glaring around him. 'Why the devil can't they realise the facts?'

'They can,' Jeff muttered. 'But the law isn't elastic enough to make allowance for them. Best thing we can do is go and see the President and thank him for reversing his decision about us.'

They crossed the crowded courtroom together to where the President was conversing with other members of the Board. At the arrival of Lance and Jeff the President turned and shook them both firmly by the hand.

'I cannot apologise enough, gentlemen,' he said, in genuine earnestness. 'We are all agreed that you must both be reinstated immediately, with salary adjustment to compensate for the miscarriage of justice.'

'That's nice to know, sir,' Lance said, 'but I think we are both facing something much more important than our former routine work. I, at least, have only one aim in life henceforth — to bring this woman Nebula to justice. I've mighty good reason, too, since she destroyed my family!'

'And I'll stick with him to the end,' Jeff declared.

'Definitely this woman is a menace,' the President admitted, 'but with the unique gifts she seems to possess I cannot see how we can possibly deal with her.'

'We're scientists,' Lance pointed out. 'It is our job in life to solve complicated mysteries — and Nebula is only one more of them. Since she has been turned loose on the world and the law cannot pin her down I consider it our bounden duty to lay some kind of plan to trap her. You, sir, as the head of the scientists, can give us every facility if you will.'

The President thought for a moment and then nodded.

'Very well. I will convene a special meeting for this evening and if you will both attend it you can outline whatever plan you have and we'll do our utmost to help.'

He glanced up as he finished speaking and added, 'Here she comes now.'

The hum of conversation ceased abruptly as Nebula became visible from the rear of the court. She was dressed in the overcoat which she had borrowed from Elsie and, presumably, was wearing the likewise borrowed frock beneath it.

Nothing could have proved more clearly that she was Nebula — but the law had no precedent for acting in a case like this.

When she reached the group of scientists she paused and raised a perfect eyebrow. Then she smiled. The bewitching beauty of her face made all the men gaze at her fixedly, and even Lance found it difficult to go on hating her. Instead he found his mind filled with all manner of vague desires. The magnetism of the woman was something that transcended all natural laws.

'I am so sorry to disappoint you, gentlemen,' she murmured, in her softest voice. 'But, after all, I am a stranger in this world of yours and I have to protect myself. I chose the easiest way of doing it — destroying my identity.'

'Then you admit you are Nebula?' Jeff snapped.

'Why not? The difficulty is for the law to prove it. And it never will . . . Do you not think I look more natural like this? That is, more like a woman of Earth? Having had the time to study them I know now what I should look like.'

'You would pass anywhere on Earth for a very beautiful woman,' Lance answered slowly. 'Only we few here know you for what you are — a creature of darkness, cruel beyond all reason, a killer. A woman who uses her beauty and wiles for only one purpose — to destroy.'

Nebula laughed slightly. 'You do not hesitate to destroy when something blocks your progress, do you?' she asked. 'Otherwise, why do you have wars?'

There was no answer. Nebula raised her shoulders lightly.

'We shall meet again, gentlemen,' she said, the fascinating blue of her eyes moving from one to the other. 'Until then I have much to do . . . '

Turning, she went on her way and vanished at length through the huge doorway. The men looked at one another.

'I am afraid,' the President said slowly, 'that many unsuspecting men are going to meet disaster at her hands — and women, too. Her personal aura is overpowering.'

'Should we follow her?' Jeff asked abruptly. 'There's no telling what she may be up to next.'

Lance shook his head. 'No use following, Jeff: she'd be up to a clumsy move like that. To peg her down we've got to devise a master plan, and we'll try and do it tonight, Mr. President, at the meeting. I've one or two theories to put forward concerning her. Once we get to the scientific root of her make-up we shall have the answer in our hands. Every disease has an antidote if one looks for it long enough.'

With that he shook hands and, with Jeff beside him, turned and left the courtroom.

★ ★ ★

There was some surprise amongst the technicians at Transmutations Limited when, early that afternoon, Lance arrived in the main laboratory. The man who had been assigned to take over his duties at the time of dismissal was busy in the control box as Lance appeared.

'Hello there, Lance!' Sid Alroyd looked up cheerfully from his scientific notes. 'Trying to drown memories of your recent ordeal by looking the old place over? I read all about the trial in the paper at midday and — '

'I've been re-instated,' Lance interrupted briefly. 'The President fixed that this morning — so from here on I take over again. You can check with him. I've a small job to do right away for him — conversion of lead into gold. You can stay with me while I do it if you like.'

'I certainly would like. I've not been given any ticklish jobs as yet; I haven't your experience. Lead into gold eh? Quite a mutation!'

Lance nodded and went across to the vacuum tube. Into it he began loading a mass of lead from the pyramids of various metals and alloys heaped against the walls. The job done he closed up the tube, checked the connections, and then came back into the control-box. He closed the switch that set up the warning light outside the door.

'That's going to turn into the hell of a lot of gold,' Alroyd said, in some surprise. 'About a hundredweight of it, I'd say.'

'About,' Lance agreed, but did not explain any further.

He closed the switches and the lighting dimmed under the sudden immense surge of power that flowed between the anode and cathode globes. For nearly ten minutes the power built up until the great laboratory was a shivering mass of colours and shattering man-made bolts of lightning. The air began to reek of ozone; the vacuum tube was hazed with the glare of atomic streamers — then slowly the disturbance died away and the dynamos whined to a standstill.

Taut-faced, Lance stepped from the control-box and hurried over to the vacuum tube. He opened the casing and smiled as he surveyed the mass of yellow metal heaped within. The transmutation was complete.

'Too heavy for me,' he said, heaving at the stuff. 'You might give me a hand to carry it down to the taxi I've got waiting outside.'

'Taxi?' Alroyd repeated blankly. 'But this mass of valuable metal will have to be checked first and — '

'I know exactly what I'm doing,' Lance interrupted. 'Give me a hand.'

He moved to a stack of cover-sheets and removed one of them, throwing it over the precious metal. Then, staggering under the weight, he and Alroyd carried the carefully camouflaged mass from the laboratory, down the corridor, and out by a side entrance. The taxi driver hopped out of his vehicle to help as the two appeared.

'What about having the stuff checked?' Alroyd demanded.

'Doesn't matter,' Lance answered, heaving the load into the rear of the taxi and then straightened up. 'The President knows all about it. Check back with him.'

'But nothing is allowed to be used or circulated without the Checking Department having particulars!'

Lance did not take any further notice. He climbed into the taxi, slammed the door, and motioned the driver to get on the move. Alroyd watched the vehicle depart down the side street and then he returned into the building vaguely puzzled. He was not quite sure what he ought to do. If he checked with the President it might look as though he was doubting Lance, who was his superior, yet on the other hand all the usual precautionary measures had been ignored.

In the finish it was early evening, and his shift in the transmutation laboratory was at an end, before Alroyd decided he ought to do something. He headed for the President's office elsewhere in the great building and to his satisfaction he heard the President's voice invite him to enter. Evidently he had not yet gone home.

Far from it. Alroyd paused in surprise as he opened the door and saw that the big office was occupied by nearly all the members of the Board. Lance himself and Jeff Walcott were also present.

'Yes, Mr. Alroyd?' the President asked expectantly being too well mannered to show he disliked being interrupted.

'Nothing, sir, it will do later.' Alroyd felt uncomfortable. 'Since Mr. Barclay is here it's all right.'

The President frowned and Lance looked surprised.

'Since *I'm* here?' he repeated. 'What has that to do with it, Sid?'

'Just checking up,' Alroyd smiled. 'You asked me to.'

'When?'

'Why — this afternoon. About the gold, remember?'

Lance looked from one man to the other. Then he got to his feet and came across the office.

'Just what are you talking about, man?' he demanded. 'I'm here for a conference and I haven't been in the building above ten minutes. Certainly I wasn't here this afternoon.'

'But — but you *were*! You said you had been reinstated and ordered to transmute that mass of lead into a hundredweight of gold. You can't have *forgotten*!'

'Since I didn't do anything of the sort I can't possibly remember it,' Lance responded. 'What was I wearing?'

'A blue suit — rather like the one you have on now.'

'This is the only navy blue suit I've got,' Lance replied bluntly. 'Anyway, go on. Tell me exactly what happened.'

Alroyd did so and at the end of the story Lance cast a significant look at the assembly.

'All right, Sid,' he said, clapping him on

the shoulder. 'It wasn't your fault for making a mistake.'

'But I *didn't* make a mistake. It *was* you. Your voice, your mannerisms, your scientific knowledge — everything. I couldn't possibly have been wrong.'

'You were, and later you'll know why,' Lance responded. 'Thanks, anyway.'

Wondering, his brows knitted, Alroyd left the office. Lance returned slowly to his chair and glanced towards the President.

'First blood to Nebula,' he said, his face taut. 'I don't have to explain what happened, do I?'

'You mean Nebula appeared as you, transmuted lead into gold for some reason best known to herself, and then vanished?' Jeff asked.

'That's it!'

'But surely it's beyond reason?' the President demanded. 'She isn't even the same sex! How could she so completely resemble you that she fooled even one of your closest associates?'

'She could because she is absolute mistress of adaptability,' Lance answered.

'I've worked out a theory on that and I'd like to explain it . . . At the moment I'm feeling sore at the fact that Nebula acted first. Obviously she transmuted the lead to gold so as to have plenty of money. Gold is still our basis of currency and with a hundredweight of it stowed away she'll have all the cash she needs. As for her imitating me: since she lived in my home for a week she had ample chance to note all my mannerisms. It wouldn't be difficult.'

Nobody said anything for a moment. The breathtaking powers of Nebula had not been thrust home so forcibly since the amazing incidents in the courtroom that morning.

'I spoke of adaptability,' Lance continued, leaning forward and looking at the circle of scientists intently. 'I base it on what I know of Nebula herself. She can change the colour of her eyes at will — as you are aware — which means she has a nervous control over the pigment causing the colour. In a very similar way the chameleon does the same thing, and the chameleon is only an animal. A creature of high reasoning power and intelligence would have a much greater range . . . On this planet of ours we have animals that are naturally camouflaged by Nature to save them from attack — the stripes of the tiger are but one instance. It is not inconceivable that a being of some other world, for Nebula must have lived on some world or other at some time, despite her assertion that she is of space itself, might have the gift of absolute adaptability. That would mean the power of being able to fit into any surroundings and change the body at will to conform with those surroundings.'

'Our greatest example of perfect adaptability lies in bacteria,' commented one of the scientists, a biologist. 'Bacteria will go on living if plunged in boiling water: they will also survive the void of interstellar space. They can exist without air, and they can change their outline at will.'

'Exactly,' Lance agreed, 'If that be so, why should not a being of Nebula's type? Because we cannot do it is no reason for saying it can't happen.'

'If we accept this theory,' the President

said slowly, 'we see how immense is our problem. If, at will, she can become somebody different on any occasion, or can exactly duplicate somebody else so no person can tell the difference, how are we ever to locate her and nail her down by our laws?'

'That is by no means the sum total of our troubles,' Lance responded, his voice grim. 'The gift of adaptability would explain her assertion that she is eternal. Probably she is in the general sense of the word since she may be able to adapt herself instantly to a bullet or a knife, and therefore experience no hurt. As a small instance, a human being such as you or I can endure boiling water on the hand if, by degrees, we have trained the hand to stand it — making the water hotter each time until one becomes adapted to it. In the same way many stage performers can absorb enormous electric voltages because they have built up a resistance through practice. In Nebula the process must be much the same, only she can do it instantly. And therein lies the danger. She is nearly incapable of being killed.'

'A most disturbing situation,' the President mused. 'The incidents of today show us what kind of a person she is.'

'She knew you were taking me back into service,' Lance pointed out, 'and so she chose her time to enter the laboratory as me, and managed to get the gold. Obviously she is a good scientist since she understood how the vacuum tube worked.'

'Yet she didn't kill Alroyd,' Jeff commented. 'I wonder what held her hand?'

'I have no idea. Perhaps she did not think he was worth the effort of destroying. I don't think Nebula destroys for the sake of it: she only does it when somebody looks likely for upsetting the smooth working of her plans.'

'What do we do to upset her plans?' Jeff demanded. 'That is the point. Alien and clever she may be, but we're not damned fools either, and we have all the resources of science at the back of us.'

'Definitely,' the President confirmed. 'The public, as yet, does not realise how dangerous Nebula is — but it will. And then there'll be trouble, unless we think of something to straighten the matter out.'

There was a long pause and everybody looked expectantly at Lance. Known to be an ingenious scientist, he seemed about the only man who could suggest something — and presently he did.

'There is one thing about Nebula which can never change,' he said, 'no matter how many changes her form takes. And that is the electrical aura that her body emanates. Every living thing has that aura, from the amoeba to the human being. It is the same energy that causes silk clothing to sometimes crackle with faint sparks in the darkness when the wearer removes them. It is the same energy that attracts another person — usually the opposite sex. Sometimes misnamed personal magnetism, it is actually electrical force. And Nebula has it in excelsis. If we could only get a reading on that aura we could build a detector that would always respond to that particular energy. In that way we should always know where she was no matter if she changed her appearance.'

'The idea's sound enough,' Jeff commented, 'but show me how we could get near enough to Nebula to ever get a reading! She'd blast hell out of us! In fact she probably will in any case because she must know that we'll be on her track from here on.'

'That,' Lance said slowly, 'is just what I'm banking on. And here is what I suggest. Tell me what you think of the plan . . .'

4

List of death

IN the heart of London there was one taxi-driver who believed he was going insane. He knew for a fact that he had picked up a man at the Research Laboratories, and that that man had seated himself in the back of the taxi beside an enormous object covered in canvas. Yet, though the taxi had not stopped en route, it was not a man who alighted from it but a woman. And a beautiful one, too, with a charming smile.

She had asked him to carry her load into the hallway of a famous hotel — and he had done so. When he asked for his fare her only response was to assure him that he did not really want it — and he believed it. So now he sat in his taxi amidst a line of vehicles and tried to fathom what in blue thunder had hit him. Where had the *man* gone? He could understand anybody changing clothes during the journey, since there was an opaque partition between back and front of the taxi, but to change from man to woman . . . ? That had him beaten, and so far he had not read of the earthquake in court.

During the late evening, however, when he returned from delivering a fare, he found Scotland Yard PC men waiting for him. The Chief Inspector briefly displayed his warrant card and then asked a question.

'You picked up a man today from the Research Laboratories about mid-afternoon. Another man who witnessed the happening — name of Alroyd — remembered the number of this taxi. Where did you take your passenger?'

'Crayley's Hotel, in the Strand — '

'He had a big, heavy package with him. Right?'

'Right. Damned near broke my back — But there's something wrong, guv'nor. I started off with a man and finished up with a woman. It's been driving me crazy trying to think how it came about. I didn't stop anywhere, see? No lights were against me, either, so I had a clean run through . . . And I didn't get paid, either. She said I didn't really want it and like an idiot I agreed with her! But I *didn't*, then — '

'You were hypnotised, my friend,' the Chief Inspector said dryly. 'And so will a lot of other people be if we don't find this woman quickly. Crayley's Hotel? Right!'

'Here,' added the Sergeant, handing over an evening paper. 'Improve your mind and see who it was you picked up.'

The two PC men returned to their police car and it whirled them to Crayley's in a matter of minutes. Since the register of names told them nothing they had to go by description — and an unforgettable blonde sounded promising. Room 4, 3rd floor.

The unforgettable blonde herself opened the door and smiled enquiringly.

'Miss — er — Sylvia Denham?' the Chief Inspector asked bluntly, glancing at the card on which he had written down the blonde's name.

'Yes, I'm Sylvia Denham. Is there

something wrong?'

The Chief Inspector stepped into the subduedly lighted room with the Sergeant behind him. The door closed. The girl with the golden hair and surprised blue eyes took a step backwards.

'I'm a police official, Miss Denham,' the C.I. explained, exhibiting his inevitable warrant card. 'From information received it appears you illegally removed a quantity of precious metal from the Research Laboratories in the City Centre this afternoon. You were disguised as a man.'

The girl said nothing, but she was smiling in what seemed genuine amusement. The Sergeant looked at her bleakly and the C.I. ran an eye over her delectable form in the close-fitting- evening gown. He had never seen a woman so devastatingly attractive.

'Do you think *I* could look like a man?' she asked dryly.

'There are reasons for believing so,' the C.I. retorted. 'We also have evidence that a woman answering your description lodged a small gold deposit in the

General Bank late this afternoon. It was after banking hours, but because of the extraordinary nature of your deposit, business was transacted. We suspect you did it by hypnotism.'

'How interesting! And what happens now?'

'I must ask you to come with me and answer a few questions. Please get your things.'

The girl did not move, but strange things began to happen to her. Hardened men though they were the Chief Inspector and Sergeant could not help a queer feeling in the stomach as they saw 'Sylvia Denham' blur and change in the most incredible fashion. Her features altered, her skin grew darker; her hair became the colour of utter night. In a matter of seconds they were looking at a woman of terrifying beauty, her scarlet orbs wide and fixed.

'My God,' the Sergeant whispered, licking his lips. 'What kind of a woman is this?'

Nebula began to move forward, her movements as sinuous as those of a reptile. When she spoke her voice had lost its gentle charm; it had a definite sibilance.

'I'll tell you what kind of a woman I am! I am a woman who is out to destroy your entire race. Destroy this whole world if need be — and what is more I have the power to do it. I am pursued by fools who haven't the slightest idea how to defeat me. And why? Because I have an intelligence ten times ahead of theirs! Amongst humans I am superhuman. As for you, my friend, and this cloddish colleague of yours, I simply find you an encumbrance, and encumbrances are best removed.'

The Chief Inspector did not say anything. He was a stolid, feet-on-the-earth policeman and though he knew he was looking straight at Death he did not flinch.

'I gather you thought to arrest me on a charge of stealing gold?' Nebula asked, and it dawned on him she was reading his mind. 'Having failed to prove my identity in any other way, this is a new angle — and completely infantile. For your information I used a fragment of the gold I stole to open an account in the Central Bank: the rest of the metal I have hidden. Later I shall use it to build up an organisation which will bring all the races of this planet to destruction! That is my avowed aim.'

The Sergeant made a slight movement towards the door and then paused as Nebula's deadly eyes pinned him. He could feel the crushing impact of her thoughts and sickness stole through him. Before he could actually collapse she switched back to the Chief Inspector.

'Back of all this I see Lance Barclay,' she said slowly. '*He* engineered this idea — just as he is engineering other ideas with the aim of encompassing my downfall. He will not succeed . . . '

Nebula turned away, musing. The Chief Inspector was perspiring so freely, his face looked as if he had just raised it from a basin of water. He knew this deadly woman — if woman she was — was just playing with him. At any moment his brain might be totally blasted and he would crash to instant death. The

Sergeant had the same notion but he knew he could not escape fast enough even if he tried.

'I shall not kill either of you,' Nebula decided suddenly, turning back to them. 'Not because I have respect for any life on this planet but because it would delay my plans if I had again to disprove my identity in court. Instead I shall allow you to leave — but henceforth neither of you will have the power of reason — !'

Her eyes opened wide, staring into the Chief Inspector's. He remained motionless but he gasped with unendurable pain as it felt as though a knife had sliced through his brain. The Sergeant, too, experienced the same deadly but brief agony. When Nebula relaxed again both men were sheet-white and shaking so much they could hardly stand.

'I think,' Nebula said, 'you will neither of you be much use to the police force any more. Now get out!'

They both moved stupidly, seeming unaware of the purpose of the open doorway. Nebula seized them, pushed them into the corridor, then slammed the door on them . . .

Other residents in the hotel saw the two blank-faced men with the drooling-mouths find their way down the staircase. Little groups watched them in amazement as they mechanically walked across the entrance hall and, as though blind, had to fumble with the outer doors. The commissionaire stared at them blankly as they half staggered to the porch.

'Anything wrong, gentlemen?' he asked in concern, and was rewarded with a vacant stare.

Fortunately for the Chief Inspector and Sergeant the constable who did the patrol car driving saw what had happened and guided both men to the vehicle. Then he drove it back to the Yard hell-for-leather and finished up half carrying the two men on either side of him as he entered the Chief Inspector's office. Within it were Lance, Jeff, the President of the Board, and Sir Arthur Dane, Assistant Commissioner of the Yard.

'In the name of the devil what's happened?' Lance cried, leaping up; then he stood watching in fascinated horror as the two men were led to the old sofa. They settled on it and looked before them, little trickles of saliva running from the corners of their mouths.

'They came out of the hotel like this,' the constable said, with a frightened glance. 'I got them here as quickly as I could.'

Sir Arthur pressed a button on the intercom. 'Send in the Divisional surgeon,' he requested, and switched off again.

Lance, his first shock over, moved to the two men and considered them fixedly, then he clenched his fists.

'If I'd have known my plan could have brought such hideousness as this I'd never have mooted it!' he said, and gave a helpless look around him. 'I knew there was danger — and so did they. But not this . . . !'

'Whatever they did was in the course of duty,' the Assistant Commissioner answered. 'They knew the risk, and took it. They went out to track down Nebula's position and give her the chance to read their minds so she could fix you as her chief enemy. Maybe she did just that: we don't know. This is how she retaliated. The point I question is: can she read minds?'

'A woman who can blast a brain with her own mind force will find telepathy child's play,' Lance retorted; then he looked up as the Divisional surgeon came into the room. He nodded to the assembly and then moved to the two helpless men sitting like babies on the sofa.

'Well?' the Assistant Commissioner asked finally, his aristocratic face grim.

'There is only one place for our two unhappy friends,' the surgeon sighed. 'An institution. Both of them are absolutely imbecile . . . ' He looked about him in the silence and added, 'I'll attend to it. They'll sit there harmlessly enough until they're removed.'

The surgeon departed quickly and Lance gave the Assistant Commissioner a bitter glance.

'We know now what we are fighting, Sir Arthur,' he said. 'We had an idea before, but this time we are sure. This Nebula is no woman: she is the greatest force for evil which ever beset this world of ours. And the longer she goes free the more difficult it will become to be rid of her. I only wish I had gone to track her down for myself — but had I done that and suffered the fate of these two worthy men here I could never have set about building a detector. It's brutal sometimes to sacrifice others to develop a plan.'

'This business goes beyond self-reproach, Barclay,' the President said. 'We're at war — and soldiers will die in the course of it. Let us hope the plan worked far enough for Nebula to know that you are her chief enemy. If she sets out to deal with you, you may yet defeat her.'

Lance nodded. 'I'd better get back home immediately just in case she starts something — as I hope. Coming Jeff?'

'Like a shot,' Jeff agreed, and with a final troubled glance at the vacant-faced men on the sofa he followed Lance to the door . . .

Meantime Nebula was still in her hotel room. In fact she was lounging on the bed, busily making notes from a copy of

Who's Who out of the hotel library. Anybody chancing to see her at this moment would only have seen an apparently ordinary though very beautiful woman. She had become blonde again and her eyes were blue. Only in the sensuous mouth with its full red lips did she betray the insensate evil that ruled her being.

Her slender hand moved over a notepad and, one by one, names appeared — and professional designations.

JAMES CARFAX, Atomic Research Engineer.
WALTER T. LANSFORD, Rocket Designer.
CALVIN THOMAS, Atlantic Tunnel Project.
ELSA CRANE, Research Worker in Rare Diseases.
HENRY MASON, Town Planner and City Architect.

Nebula worked on her list until well after midnight, by which time the hotel had become quiet. Then, memorising the list by reading it through once she set fire to it, rose from the bed, and went to the wardrobe for the overcoat and hat she had bought in the hotel shopping centre that afternoon.

She left the room silently, and the hotel itself by the night hall, taking her key with her. Outside, the night porter summoned a taxi for her.

'I want Dale Road, Hampstead,' she instructed the driver. 'You can drop me at the end of the street.'

'Very good, miss.'

Throughout the journey Nebula remained in thoughtful mood in the back of the vehicle, until finally it came to regions she recognised from her stay with the Barclays. In accordance with her orders the driver pulled up at the end of Dale Road and opened the door for her.

'Wait for me,' she said. 'I shall not be long.'

The taxi driver saluted and returned to the wheel. Nebula walked almost in silence under the leaf-bare trees, glancing about her. Most of the houses in the road were in darkness but here and there a light glowed behind a bedroom window. When she reached No. 47 she paused and surveyed it for a moment. It was in complete darkness.

Opening and closing the gate silently she kept well within the few trees lining the front path. By this means, and knowing the layout of the house and gardens so intimately, she reached the French windows of the lounge within a few moments. To open them by means of a glass-cutter and suction cup was simple; then she stepped silently into the thick darkness of the room beyond.

There were no sounds. Drawing out a torch she switched it on and flashed the beam around her. The room was quite empty of people. Crossing it, she went out into the hall and up the familiar staircase. At the room that had been her own she listened attentively, but there were no sounds. In the rooms on either side of it, however, she could hear the deep breathing of a man in each case.

Without a sound she opened the door of the left-hand room and crept within. Like a ghost she went to the bed and looked down on Jeff, fast asleep. She hesitated, then went out again. In the right-hand room Lance was sprawled under the bedclothes, his face in profile, his chest rising and falling: rhythmically. Nebula studied him for a moment or two, her lips drawn back from her teeth in vicious hate. She did not use her torch in case the beam disturbed him: in any event the starlight was bright enough through the uncurtained window to allow her to see him.

In the gloom her blue eyes changed to red and, in the dimness, looked like those of a cat catching light reflection, except that the glow was scarlet instead of emerald. Lance twisted uneasily and then suddenly his breathing ceased. He became motionless.

Silently Nebula withdrew, and left the house like a ghost, returning to her taxi and giving instructions to be driven back to the hotel. She was not aware that from the dark window of Lance's bedroom two men were watching her departure. When the taxi had vanished from sight, Jeff switched on the lights and mopped his face.

'I hope I don't ever have to go through that again!' he declared. 'She found me first, and I thought it was all up. Why she didn't kill me I don't know.'

'Because, as I've said before, she doesn't kill without a reason,' Lance answered. 'When you become a menace to her she'll single you out. As she did me . . . ' and for a moment he grinned as he looked at the bed.

Lying in the clothes was a plastic model of himself — as far as the head and shoulders and trunk were concerned. The face, however, exactly duplicated his own — a synthetic mask, easy enough to make in the laboratory after the fashion of a death mask. The hair was false yet indistinguishable from the real thing. In fact the image in the bed was Lance, except to those who had reason to know differently.

'If she'd have switched on a torch she might have gathered the trick,' Jeff commented, tightening the girdle about his dressing gown.

'I don't think so, Jeff: chiefly because she wouldn't be expecting such a gag.

Anyway, the idea worked. I had my eye on her all the time whilst I was concealed in the wardrobe there — and I think the detector worked okay. We can soon see.'

Lance reached under the bed and brought forth a circular object that looked like a cross between a compass and stopwatch. Around it were small horse-shoe magnets. He pressed the master-switch and then whistled in delight as the immobile needle suddenly swung round to a number and remained fixed.

'We've got it!' he cried. 'And what an aura that woman has! Look at the electronic rating — up to seventy-two! That is twenty times higher than any normal person.'

Jeff nodded, familiar enough with the instrument to know what it had done. It had been placed under the bed because Nebula would presumably head for the bed when entering the room. Whichever side of the bed she had chosen, the detector had power enough to absorb whatever aura she was emanating and store it up in its self-contained battery. Now the absorbed power was released it automatically registered itself.

'Which gives us a constant line on her,' Lance continued, his eyes gleaming. 'She also thinks she has killed me off, which is a great help. She won't be expecting anything from me. I wasn't sure what method she would use to wipe me out, but I judged it would be mind force — and I was correct. I guessed what she was up to when she stood concentrating at the bedside. So I died convincingly.'

He threw back the bedclothes and looked down on his plastic body. To it was attached an air tube which, concealed under the carpet, had led back to the wardrobe. A pair of bellows had been all that was necessary to produce the rise and fall of a breathing effect. The apparent movement upon 'death' taking place had been created by the deflation of air that had caused the image to move slightly.

'Well, we've got tabs on her all right, even if two worthy men of the law were blasted into insanity to tempt Nebula this far,' Jeff commented. 'But wouldn't it have been quicker to capture her whilst she was here?'

Lance sighed. 'How long is it going to take you, Jeff, to realise that we're not dealing with an ordinary woman? We could have captured her very easily, but how much good would it have done us? If she hadn't blasted us by mind force we would have got her as far as a courtroom, maybe. Then what? Change of identity and release. Same old story . . . On the other hand, if we'd tried to kill her — shooting or stabbing perhaps, she'd have survived either or both. I'm convinced of it. No, this is the best way. Keep track of her and work out our plan a stage further. When we *do* nail her she has got to be so tied up she cannot possibly escape.'

'She'll always have her mind force,' Jeff pointed out. 'One look from her eyes when she's in a corner and we're done for.'

'I know. Her eyes are her weapons. But what happens if they are covered with a shield, which no radiation can penetrate? She will be a Samson shorn of her hair. However, that is in the future. Our job is to get a compass made to operate on this particular aura, and it must be sensitive enough to reach for several thousand miles — in fact anywhere on Earth where Nebula is likely to go. Once we know where she is we can work gradually to trap her. The other thing we have to do is get the publicity hounds to work proclaiming my death in mysterious circumstances. And you keep a lookout for yourself, Jeff! Her next move may be to find you since she knows you are — or were my best friend.'

5

The detector

The following morning 'Sylvia Denham' left Crayley's Hotel for parts unknown. Scotland Yard, still on the alert traced her movements as far as Victoria Station — and after that she completely disappeared. Probably because Scotland Yard was watching for a beautiful blonde and failed to find one once she had boarded the train. In a word, Nebula utterly vanished.

Meantime, the general public had read with regret of the 'mysterious death' of Lance Barclay — but the public being what it is, daily life went on just as usual. No reference was made to Nebula, the scientists and the law preferring to suppress all information about her so they could work unhindered . . .

And behind closed doors in the research laboratories Lance was supervising the creation of a super-sensitive detector, backed by all the resources of science, his helpers — amongst whom Jeff was chief of staff — being sworn to secrecy. But, whilst the detector was being made, Nebula was on the move — and Lance chafed accordingly. The detector was such a highly delicate instrument and required such complicated assembly it could not possibly be ready under seven days.

And in that time?

Only the law could hope to keep on Nebula's trail — or at least do its best to do so. To the office of the Assistant Commissioner there came reports at intervals. Large bank accounts had been opened in various cities throughout England — by a different person on each occasion. Other different people had bought up derelict land and had machinery and equipment delivered there. A firm of constructional engineers was busy building an underground factory, working under sealed orders. Since nothing was sealed to the law the managing director of the firm had to state from whom he had received his orders — and answered that his customer was a frail, grey-haired man of middle age. So Scotland Yard scratched its fact-bound head and wondered what was going to happen next.

Down in a remote part of Surrey a brilliant young atomic research engineer by the name of James Carfax was far too busy with his experiments to pay much attention to what was happening in the outer world. He had been given this quaint old deserted house, and every facility, to pursue his research, the Board of Scientists feeling that, given his head, he would open up new fields in atomic power. James Carfax, aged 25, was in fact the Faraday of his particular time.

In spite of his technical brilliance, however, 'Jimmy' Carfax was still human being enough to be in love. When he was not brooding in his laboratory of scientific gadgets and thinking up new uses for atomic power, he was discussing them with Margaret. Margaret, of the chestnut hair and smiling eyes, believed in him. She knew he would get around to marrying her when Project X9 was complete — Project X9 being the use of atomic power for industrial purposes, with every possible danger removed. In fact Project X9 was what all civilisation was waiting for. It would bring the coal and gas era to an end and advance mankind one long stride on the road to ultimate perfection.

Margaret lived in the village only two miles from Jimmy Carfax's 'lair'. He had known her for three years and only exchanged views with her because he knew she was implicitly to be trusted — and anyway she was not scientist enough to repeat anything of the technicalities. Margaret, in fact, was the only girl permitted to enter the 'lair' outside of the specially chosen man-servant who did all the ordinary jobs from cooking meals to holding gadgets whilst the young genius experimented.

It was about four days after the disappearance of Nebula from the Crayley Hotel that Margaret made her usual evening call on Jimmy, the dour-faced manservant admitting her with a taciturn greeting. Margaret, rosy-cheeked from the cold autumn air, her saucy beret one-sided on her chestnut-coloured hair, made her way along the hall and into the laboratory. She knocked, and waited.

'Come in, come in,' Jimmy sang out, then he looked surprised as Margaret entered, loosening her overcoat as the warmth of the place struck her.

'What's the idea of knocking?' Jimmy asked in surprise coming over and embracing her. 'Surely you know that you're welcome?'

'Of course — but you might have been doing something tricky and I *could* have spoiled it!'

'Always considerate!' Jimmy laughed, kissing her dimpled cheek. 'You'd make the perfect laboratory assistant.'

'If I wanted. Personally I don't think I'd like it. Too many gadgets — and, at times, too many horrible smells.'

Jimmy grinned, and it made him look more boyish than ever. Despite twenty-five years he had the appearance of being in his teens. Probably it was caused by his lean fresh-complexioned face and tousled fair hair. He stood looking at Margaret for a moment and saw her brown eyes surveying the instruments.

'Got any further since I was last here?' she asked.

'That was only last evening, anyway. What do you think I am — a magician?'

'In some things,' Margaret said, and they both laughed.

Then Jimmy became thoughtful again. He drew up a chair for the girl and contented himself with half sitting on the edge of the untidy wall-bench.

'I'm making good progress,' he said. 'In fact, before many more weeks have gone I think Project X9 will be an established fact. I've sent in reports of my progress to the Board of Scientists and they're highly satisfied. As I've told you many a time, atomic power has so many uses, besides being destructive.'

'You've told me, yes, but I haven't understood you. I think I was born without a scientific kink.'

'Which is probably why I love you. A scientific woman is somehow — er — ' Jimmy did not commit himself to an observation; instead he switched back to his topic. 'Everything has a by-product,' he explained. 'Coal-tar, gunpowder, plastics, acids, anything you can mention, has *other* uses besides the basic one originally intended. Offshoots, as it were. So it is with atomic force. Quite cheaply, if used in certain quantities — which I'm working on right now — it can light a city for a negligible cost. It can drive liners, trains, road vehicles, and airplanes. It can fling spaceships across the void, superseding dangerous rocket fuels. But it can also become the basis for new metals, building materials, and clothes. The shattering of the atom, in fact, produces an endless chain of new states of matter. One aspect of it is transmutation of elements, as used at Transmutations Limited, but it is only one aspect. My own researches open up a practically infinite field . . . '

Jimmy stopped and gave an apologetic smile. 'All of which you find incredibly boring, of course. I should know better.'

'Boring? No!' Margaret shook her head. 'I find it very interesting. And the Board of Scientists knows every detail of this project, I suppose?'

'Not yet. It isn't complete — but it will

be before long. When that happens you can watch Mankind stride forward into a new era of cheap power and endless achievement.'

'In fact you are a world-builder?' Margaret smiled. 'And you look so young, too!'

'I *am* young — but it's the work that counts. If I achieve my object before I'm thirty, all the better for me. I can dabble for the rest of my life — if you'll put up with it.'

Margaret laughed and rose from the chair. 'After what I've seen here I can put up with anything.'

She kissed Jimmy gently as he half perched on the bench and then she strolled around the laboratory, surveying the equipment. Jimmy watched her, pleased by her interest. On other occasions she had always seemed glad to escape from the vast variety of electrical and atomic gadgets that loomed in all directions.

'And Mankind will stride forward into a new era of cheap power and endless achievement,' Margaret repeated at last, turning.

'That's it! I consider myself destined to do it — and sometimes I find it an overwhelming thought.'

Margaret came back to where Jimmy was standing. Her brown eyes looked into his intently and he smiled at her — then his expression began to change. For a moment he was not sure whether or not it was a trick of the lights, but Margaret's eyes did not look quite the same. They were changing colour as if lambent fires had been kindled in their depths.

'Margaret — what's the matter?'

Jimmy caught hold of the girl firmly, then as the metamorphosis of her eyes became complete he suddenly realised that he was in deadly danger. This was not the Margaret of the winsome smile and carefree ways. It was — He just didn't know. He swung round dazedly and snatched at a trimming knife on the bench behind him.

Whirling round he drove it down hard, not with any vicious action but because he knew his life depended on it. The blade buried itself to the hilt in the girl's breast. She staggered a little from the impact, but that was all,

Her eyes opened wider, and wider still, until all Jimmy Carfax's world seemed to be made up of red orbs. He could not see anything or feel anything else. He was floundering on the edge of destruction — and at last he went over, crashing on to the floor.

Nebula looked down at him then tugged the knife from her breast and contemplated the shining blade. It was slightly blood-streaked. She tossed it on the floor in contempt, then moving across to the wall mirror she tugged off her coat and opened the dress as far as the wound. The only visible sign of it, even though it had struck directly to her heart, was a rapidly healing scar. By the time she had wiped away the blood traces with a piece of clean rag even the scar had gone.

A few minutes later she left the laboratory. The manservant glided to the front door to open it for her.

'Good night, Miss Harrison,' he said politely.

'Good night, Benson,' Nebula responded. 'Oh — don't disturb Mr. Carfax for the next hour. He's doing a very intricate job and asked me to tell you.'

'Very good, miss.'

And Nebula stepped out into the night . . . An hour later the nude body of a girl was found two miles from the Carfax house by a farm worker crossing one of the fields from a late session of calfing. He promptly informed the police and they in turn had the body identified as that of Margaret Harrison. About the same time Benson discovered his young master lying dead on the laboratory floor, a look of utter imbecility on his features.

It was not long before Scotland Yard had the facts, and the most troubled man in that organisation was undoubtedly the Assistant Commissioner. Despite the fact that it took them from vital work on the detector, he summoned Lance and Jeff to his office to give them the details. The President of the Board of Scientists went with them.

'Nebula again, obviously,' Lance said bitterly. 'She must have learned that Carfax was one of the most promising scientists of the day. Then she found his nearest associate — his girlfriend in this case — and took her place.'

'And wiped out the one man who could have advanced civilisation immeasurably,' the President said pinching finger and thumb to his eyes.

'From the very start we have that one factor in Nebula to contend with,' Lance said. 'For a reason unexplained she hates the Earthly race, and is out to destroy it. That means that wherever she can she will wipe out any man or woman who looks likely for helping the race to advance. And she's made a good start with Carfax. He was a most valuable man.'

'When I think of the many key men and women who are advancing us I shudder to think what may happen,' the Assistant Commissioner said. 'And it's impossible to guard all of them. The only thing I can do is throw everything into the effort of having my men trying to trace her movements.'

'You'll never do it, sir,' Lance said bluntly. 'Already, following this Carfax business, she's vanished completely. Only our detector can trace her, and that will take another two days to complete. Let us hope nothing else of a serious nature happens in that two days . . . Come on, Jeff, we'd better get back and rush things all we can.'

So they returned to the laboratory and urged the men working for them to all possible effort. Meantime the Yard did its best to get a line on Nebula, and failed completely — the reason being her ability to change her appearance at will. With that factor in the way even the most trained investigator was utterly beaten.

In the next two days there were no visible signs of Nebula's activities, but there *were* other things in the general order of the country, which suggested a malignant hand somewhere. Strikes, almost unheard of in these modern times, suddenly began to reappear. Nor were they isolated instances. They seemed to happen simultaneously and affected docks, transport and food delivery stations. In one day all these necessary utilities came to a standstill, and on the day afterwards they were followed by wider strikes in power stations, supply depots and news centres. The whole nervous system of the country, in fact, was being paralysed and those at the head of the strikes declared flatly that their reason for action was the need for better conditions and pay.

In this respect the Yard had better luck. They were able to trace the strikes to one ultimate source. Every agent, it seemed, had received orders, and was carrying them out. Each agent spoke of a different mastermind in the background, but there was little doubt but what it was Nebula, operating from some hidden spot. The underground factory that the Yard knew had been built was visited — and apparently was a photographic storage depot with a doddering old man in charge of it. He refused to say who his employer was and all the efforts of the Yard could not trace him, either.

'Will it stop here? That is the point,' the Assistant Commissioner declared, as he and the President of the Board of Scientists discussed the matter in Whitehall. 'Having brought nearly all public services to a standstill in this country I am expecting that her next move will be to involve other countries abroad. Certainly our own strike-leaders will not listen to reason, and all the terms we've suggested make no impression. So apparently Nebula is carrying out her aim to smash up our civilisation entirely.'

'If only I knew why!' The President banged the desk in exasperation. 'It is bad enough to have one woman upsetting the entire social order of a country, but not to know *why* she does it is even worse — '

He paused as the 'phone rang. The Assistant Commissioner raised it.

'Yes? Assistant Commissioner here . . . ' He became intent. 'Yes. Yes, right away. We'll be there.'

He switched off and looked up eagerly. 'Those two boys of yours have got the detector finished — and it's working! We'd better go over and take a look at it immediately.'

The President got to his feet hurriedly and in five minutes a patrol car had whirled them to the laboratories. In three minutes more they were in the laboratory studying a device about as large as a big goldfish bowl, and not unlike it in appearance.

'This is it, gentlemen,' Lance said. 'You see the needle poised? At the moment it is pointing directly to wherever Nebula is. The needle is energised so as to respond to an aura identical to hers, so of course it does not pick out anybody else *but* her. It will only drop to zero and become useless if she dies — and from the way things are going that can't be too soon. The whole device is sealed inside a vacuum to give absolute freedom of action to the needle. This button here operates this indicator and gives us the distance away of Nebula from the needle-point. That is arrived at by the strength of the aura being received. Thus . . . '

Lance pressed the button he had indicated and the electronic calculator, controlled entirely by the amount of aura energy it received through an amplifying transformer, began to whirr. In a small glass window figures appeared and became steady.

'Forty-eight miles, due south,' the President said. 'That is nearly on the coast.'

'And it is also where that underground factory was put up,' the Assistant Commissioner pointed out. 'I'll swear that place is her headquarters if we could only nail her in them. It lies in the Downland not far from Worthing — '

'Wait!' Jeff interrupted. 'She's on the move — and the distance is increasing.'

Fascinated, the men and laboratory technicians watched the brilliant instrument that was tracking the movements of the mystery woman. The indicator shifted position until it pointed more to the south-east. The numbers began to increase rapidly on the mileage-indicator.

'She's heading south-east at a mighty rapid rate, and the velocity is increasing,' Lance said, frowning. 'Wonder what game she's up to now?'

'South-east will take her over the African continent,' the President said. 'And from the speed the miles are increasing at she's using an aeroplane of the fastest type. But where is she *going*?'

There was a puzzled silence for a moment, then the President gave a start.

'Great heavens, I hope I'm wrong!' he

exclaimed. 'But out near Kinshasa in Zaire there's one of our greatest workers on bacteria — Elsa Crane. She's been there for four years and more, as valuable to the science of medicine as Carfax was to atomics. If this devil Nebula gets hold of her — '

'You've hit it, sir!' Lance declared, his eyes hard. 'And we've got to act fast. This compass-indicator is portable so we can mount it in a jet-plane and head after Nebula right away. She's got to be stopped on her rampage of destruction even if we ourselves get killed in the doing. Give orders right away, sir, for a plane to be made ready, and I'll fly it myself,' then at the President's surprised look he added: 'I'm a qualified pilot.' Then he began the task of unbolting the detector from its temporary mounting.

★ ★ ★

Elsa Crane was a woman of middle-age, and one of the most advanced bacteriologists in the profession. Because of her researches in the torrid, fever-infested regions of central West Africa she had brought to the science of medicine cures for some of the most deadly diseases. Cancer was almost mastered thanks to her efforts and other ills also looked likely for falling before her relentless probing into their causes.

Frail in appearance, yet possessed of the devouring energy of a creator, Elsa Crane lived only for her work with the test tube and microscope. The crushing heat, the circumscribed limits of her tropical base camp, the few Europeans and natives who were true to her cause . . . she knew little else. And needed little else. Which was a good enough reason for her being surprised when her radio equipment tuned on a secret waveband to London — chiefly for the purpose of her transmitting valuable medical secrets — came to life in her laboratory and issued a warning.

'Scotland Yard speaking, Miss Crane,' said the voice from London, after she had acknowledged she was receiving the reception. 'You are warned to be on your guard against a visitor. We cannot say what her appearance will be like — or even if she will be a woman at all. She may be a man. But the fact remains that we believe you are in danger. Do not admit any strangers.'

'But what is the *reason* for this?' Elsa Crane demanded in amazement. 'What is Scotland Yard doing to allow a dangerous visitor to come looking for me?'

'The details are too involved to explain at the moment, Miss Crane, and you are too out of touch with the ordinary world to wish to be bothered with them. Just be on your guard; that is all. Goodbye.'

So with that Elsa Crane had to be satisfied — but she was not the only one who had received the message. Nebula had received it, too, using a radio equipment which made mockery of all secret wavebands. Her 'plane, too, was utterly unorthodox, flashing through the highest stratosphere at fantastic speed and using only the atomic power of pure water for its fuel. The breakdown of the oxygen and hydrogen atoms produced enough energy to fling the amazing craft through the sky, or even space itself, at breathtaking speed. Certainly there was no jet-plane anywhere that would be able to catch up with her.

At the moment she was high above Algeria and speeding southwards. Her plane made no noise and left no exhaust trail, so all normal means of tracing it were useless. She, for her part, as the President had guessed, was on her way to deal with the foremost woman in medical science — Elsa Crane, and to detect Elsa in the wastes of the central Africa was no problem. She, like everyone else, had an aura wavelength, but to Nebula detecting such a wavelength was not a matter of knowing the aura first. She had instead a vastly improved version of Lance's detector, which reacted to light-photons as well as energy. In other words its needle responded to the waves given off by a white female, the female having a higher wavelength than the male, and since there could hardly be more than one white female in these wastes at the moment the matter presented no problem.

But this warning did, and Nebula

frowned over it as she watched the wilderness of Algeria slowly give place to the blurred green of the African forests far below. It was mid-afternoon and the furious heat of the African sun was etching the terrain below with the sharpness of acid.

But Nebula was not at a loss for long. She flew on until her detector gave her the approximate position of Elsa Crane, then she descended silently from the heights and finally alighted in a clearing. Here she locked the controls of her strange machine and climbed out into the jungle, armed with a gun which certainly had no counterpart in modern civilisation. She knew she might have wild beasts to deal with, and if her mental power was not quick enough to slay them with, a gun was the only answer. She also knew that, since warning had gone on ahead to Elsa Crane, Scotland Yard had somehow discovered her intentions — and the thought did not please her in the least.

Elsa Crane herself, true to instructions, gave orders that no visitors were to be permitted within the palisaded confines of the research camp — but as it happened no visitors arrived. Then, as the tropical night was closing down there crept into the forest silence the hum of jetplane motors and eventually the plane itself came flying out of the darkness, searchlights guiding it, and landed on the flat field at the rear of the camp. A few minutes later Elsa Crane found herself shaking hands with the President of the Board of Scientists, the Assistant Commissioner, Lance, and Jeff.

'Much as I appreciate the warning, gentlemen,' she said, leading the way into the low-walled living room, 'I'm afraid you miscalculated somewhere. Nobody has been here — nor in fact has there been any trace of anybody.'

'Our detector shows that an enemy is quite near, Miss Crane,' the President said. 'Not more than two miles away in the jungle. We intend to set out after her immediately but we thought we had better let you know first what was happening.'

'What *is* happening?' the bewildered bio-chemist asked, spreading her hands.

'I'm utterly in the dark.'

So the President told the full story over refreshment, then when it was over he got to his feet.

'Our job,' he said quietly, 'is now to find this thing, this woman, and obliterate her somehow. And it must be done immediately. We'll return afterwards . . . If you are ready, gentlemen?'

The others nodded and followed him from the bungalow and into the clearing again. They headed across its gloomy darkness to the deserted plane and clambered within to begin the task of unbolting the detector and carrying it with them.

Lance switched on the lights, then almost immediately he paused, staring in horrified amazement. He did not need to say anything; the others saw what he had seen at the same moment. The detector-compass had been smashed to fragments! Its vacuum case lay in curved shards of glass on the floor and the delicate instrument within, into which had gone so many hours of endeavour, was a tangled ruin of torn wires, bent metal, and broken springs.

'Where *is* she?' Jeff breathed murderously, clenching his fists. 'Let me get at her for this! I'll — '

'No use going off half-cocked, Jeff,' Lance interrupted him, moving forward to inspect the ruin. 'We should have had more sense than leave the 'plane unguarded. It never occurred to me — since our last reading showed Nebula was two miles away — that she'd ever come across our flyer.'

'Well she has, and she isn't far away,' Jeff snapped. 'I'd better head back to the bungalow and keep an eye on Miss Crane. Anything might happen now.'

He left the cabin and jumped into the clearing. Lance turned and looked at the President and the Assistant Commissioner.

'Which, for the time being, ruins all our chances of finding where Nebula is,' the President said bitterly. 'What utter idiots we were!'

'We can build another detector, but it will take time,' Lance said. 'In any case it will have to wait for the moment. Our immediate job is to see if we can locate her anywhere in the jungle. She can't be very far away. Jeff is watching the bungalow, so we'll do the rest. Come on.'

He hurried outside, his revolver ready for action even though he knew it would probably not prove of much use against the super-adaptive girl. Glancing towards the bungalow he failed to see any signs of disturbance; then he turned to the President and the Assistant Commissioner.

'No use us staying in a group,' he said. 'You two gentlemen take different routes, and I'll go this way. We'll meet again here later. If any of us see Nebula we shoot — and no questions asked. She's as dangerous as any wild animal.'

With that he hurried into the wilderness of vegetation and began to search in the midst of it, using his torch at intervals. He had the hope that, even if he did not come upon the girl herself he might at least get some idea of where her camp was — or her airplane — after which it might be possible to lie in wait for her.

But there were no clues anywhere, and though he marked the trees to guide him back, Lance did not penetrate too far into the wilderness for fear of losing himself. He returned to the clearing to find the President and Assistant Commissioner had already returned, with nothing to report.

'Waste of time,' the Assistant Commissioner said briefly. 'Looking for Nebula in the African jungle is worse than looking for the needle in the haystack. So we'd better — '

He paused and turned expectantly as Jeff came hurrying across the clearing from the bungalow.

'Any luck?' he enquired, coming up, then as the three shook their heads he said, 'Nothing's happened here, either — but that doesn't alter the fact that Nebula's somewhere about. I think we should get in the 'plane, switch on all the searchlights, then toothcomb the jungle below in the glare.'

'With foliage intervening that won't be too easy,' Lance pointed out.

'I'd thought of that, but it's unlikely

that her 'plane — for she must certainly have used one — will be hidden by trees. She's bound to have landed in an open space. Suppose we take a look anyway?'

'And if Miss Crane is attacked in the meantime?' the Assistant Commissioner asked.

'I hardly see how she can be. Her native staff — all powerful men used to the jungle — know exactly what is threatening. Nebula wouldn't stand any chance against them, no matter how subtle she was.'

'All right,' Lance decided, after brief thought, 'we'll see if we can find anything.'

They returned to the 'plane, closed the cabin door, and Lance took over the controls. In a matter of minutes he had forced the machine over the treetops and turned to switch on the external searchlights. Then he paused as a woman's voice spoke.

'Never mind the searchlights, Lance. You won't need them.'

Lance had the presence of mind to switch on the automatic pilot before turning round in his seat — then he gazed fixedly at Nebula, dressed in Jeff's clothing, her peculiar weapon in her right hand. On the other side of the control room the Assistant Commissioner and President were looking at her in fixed incredulity.

'I certainly have no doubts any more that the people of Earth are fools,' Nebula stated. 'You left the door wide open for me when you went probing into the jungle. Naturally, after reaching your 'plane and wrecking the detector, I kept very close at hand to see what you did. In the bungalow I had only Jeff, Elsa Crane, and a few servants and workers to deal with. It was simple. I attracted Jeff outside by a slight sound, and then dealt with him. From that moment afterwards, in his clothes, I *was* him — and nobody knew the difference. Not even Elsa Crane. I gather, Lance, I didn't kill you after all.'

'And Miss Crane?' Lance asked tautly.

'Is that so difficult to imagine? I came to Africa for the sole purpose of eliminating her. I would hardly leave without accomplishing my mission. You were fools to take my suggestion that we fly away from the bungalow: had you examined it you would have found Miss Crane within, dead in her laboratory. In the jungle nearby is Jeff's body.'

Goaded beyond endurance Lance jumped to his feet and lashed out his fist at the girl. Since she wasn't expecting it she took the blow on the side of her head and staggered a little. Lance jumped forward to follow up his advantage, but Nebula's gun jerked up quickly and stopped him.

'One more move like that, Lance, and I'll kill you!' she warned, her enormous violet eyes merging into redness

'Why don't you anyway?' Lance demanded recklessly. 'That's all you really aim to do, isn't it?'

'Not altogether — even though it may be my eventual aim. I want you to know my purpose. A victory is very empty without somebody to share it.'

'What victory?' demanded the President, and the boring eyes turned to him.

'I am talking about my victory over the fools who populate this planet. You know as well as I do that you cannot possibly defeat me. I have already thrown much of

Britain into chaos — thanks to the army of agents I have working for me, most of them under post-hypnotic orders. My plans are such that before I have finished I will have other countries likewise paralysed. Out of paralysis of social services there can only grow one thing — war. And that I intend to foment.'

'Why?' Lance muttered. 'What heinous purpose is behind your utterly ruthless campaign against us?'

Nebula did not answer the question: she went on talking.

'War I can as easily foment as I can strikes. With my power to resemble anybody on Earth I choose I can walk into the secret chambers of the heads of every country. I can spread such stories that war will be inevitable — and with the unreasoning blindness which Earthlings possess, together with their stocks of scientifically destructive weapons, a war such as the planet has never known could possibly blow the whole Earth to pieces. If that happened I would be satisfied. I should consider it my crowning achievement.'

Lance's gaze dropped to Nebula's gun.

She had unconsciously lowered it whilst speaking.

'None of this makes sense, Nebula,' he said. 'That you hate Earthlings is obvious, but there must be a reason.'

Still she did not answer the question.

'You men — and Jeff whilst he lived — have hounded me from the very moment I was re-born in that vacuum-tube — that is why I want you to witness my crowning victory when I have put nation against nation and brother against brother. That would be recompense indeed . . . For that reason I do not wish to kill you. I prefer to take you back to my hidden headquarters, there to remain until the great day when I have accomplished my end.'

The gun was even lower as the girl dreamily reflected, her eyes turning to a soft, lambent blue again. The plane, automatically controlled, flew on steadily.

'For the last time,' Lance said deliberately, 'why do you hate us so?'

'Because you are the descendants of the race who slew my race and destroyed my world!'

139

Lance was genuinely puzzled, and looked it.

'When did that happen?' he asked. 'We can't be expected to remember it. It must have been somewhere in the dim antiquity of time.'

'Count the planets in the System and think it out for yourself,' Nebula retorted.

'Mercury, Venus, Earth, Mars,' the President said, naming the planets in progression from the sun. 'Jupiter Saturn, Uranus, Neptune, and — if it still counts as a planet — Pluto . . . Well, what about them?' he asked, shrugging.

'You missed one!' Nebula's voice was venomous as she looked at him. 'It was the world of Nimatus when I and my race lived upon it. Now it is in ruins — thanks to your progenitors! It used to lie between the orbits of Mars and Jupiter. Your own astronomers wonder what happened to blow it to bits. I *know* what happened, and I mean to exact full payment because the laws of chance have given me that opportunity!'

'The asteroids!' Lance cried, starting. 'Is that the world you mean? Or rather the remains of one?'

'You know as well as anybody else with astronomical knowledge that the asteroids are the remains of a missing planet in the System! I lived on that world countless cycles ago. I was living on it when it fell to pieces and I was plunged into death by disintegration. Nothing else could have destroyed me — or my race — for we were eternal. Just as I am eternal again now . . . But why should I tell you all this?' Nebula asked, half to herself.

'So that we can witness your victory, didn't you say?' Lance asked in contempt; then seeing her attention had strayed from her gun he abruptly slammed out his fist with all his power. It struck Nebula on the side of the jaw and sent her spinning backwards against the curved wall. Her gun dropped from her hand. Another blow battered her to her knees and before she could get up again Lance had pinned her wrists half way up her back.

'Get some wire,' he ordered curtly, regardless of the fact that the President and Assistant Commissioner were his superiors. 'Now we've got this wild-cat we're sticking to her. Much as I dislike knocking a woman about this is one occasion when I've got to.'

Nebula fought and struggled savagely, but her strength was not sufficient to defeat Lance, and since he kept behind her she could not use her deadly eyes on him either. Finally her wrists and ankles had been tightly fastened with spare flex and Lance threw her face downwards on the bunk.

'You're best in that position, where you can't look at us,' he told her, as she squirmed and writhed helplessly. 'I don't quite know what we're going to do with you, but I do know we are not going to lose you.'

And with that he turned back to the controls and set the machine's course for England.

6

Captured

Against the three determined men Nebula had no chance, and for extra precaution they blindfolded her with wadding so there was no opportunity for her to use her most lethal weapon. Thuswise, guided between the President and Lance, with the Assistant Commissioner coming up in the rear, she was led from the 'plane at the airport and taken to an official car for which the Assistant Commissioner had sent forth an advance radio order whilst the 'plane had been flying.

And that was where he had made his mistake, apparently, for before very long it dawned on Lance that the car was not going into the centre of London towards Whitehall, where Nebula was to be charged, but away from the city. In a matter of minutes it struck a country road and opened up to an effortless 75 miles an hour.

'What the devil's the idea?' Lance demanded of the driver. 'Get back to London — and quickly!'

'You can save your breath, Lance,' Nebula said, turning her blindfolded face towards him. 'This is only one of the many hundreds of agents I have who keep a watch on my safety. When the Assistant Commissioner sent out a radio call for a car to meet him because he had captured me my agents would pick it up. You can imagine the rest. The genuine car would be ditched and the driver wiped out. At the moment you are going where I wish, not where you wish.'

'Like hell we are!' Lance retorted, snatching out his automatic and levelling it. 'Turn this car round immediately.'

The driver took no notice and the car continued its high speed through the country lanes in the bright autumnal sunlight.

'This car is not like an ordinary one,' Nebula explained. 'If you shoot the driver and he loses control of the vehicle it will instantly blow up, killing you immediately. It will not kill me because I can adapt myself to anything except total disintegration and the explosive is not powerful enough to cause that.'

'A lot of damned bluff!' the Assistant Commissioner declared angrily, and at that the girl laughed slightly.

'Is it? You have only to try to prove it.'

If it was bluff it was clever. To try and prove it was to risk death. And on the other hand . . . ?

Lance saw that the car was approaching a sharp bend ahead and came to a sudden decision.

'Since this driver can't lose control of the vehicle without blowing himself and everybody else to bits he can't interfere with us, either. We're getting out — and you're going first, Nebula. See if you can adapt yourself to a fall on concrete at seventy-five miles an hour!'

The Assistant Commissioner and President exchanged startled glances, but by that time Lance had acted. He snapped open the door, seized the girl by the shoulders, then bundled her out neck and crop. A few seconds after, as the car began to break for the approaching bend,

Lance himself took a running leap and crashed over and over into the dry ditch at the roadside. Looking back after the speeding car and paining with bruises he saw the door close as, evidently, the Assistant Commissioner and President did not choose to take such desperate risks at their more mature age.

Lance got slowly to his feet and returned along the road to where Nebula was squirming savagely to tear loose from her wire bonds. To Lance's amazement there was not even a scratch visible on her body though the suit of Jeff's she was wearing was ripped in several places from the impact with the roadway. He hauled her to her feet and kept a grip on her.

'Take this thing from my eyes,' she ordered fiercely. 'At least give me the chance to see where I'm going!'

'Why should I? I'm not giving you the opportunity to work some of your filthy brain-blasting tricks. The only place you are going is back to London, even if we have to walk all the way. Now get moving.'

Instead of obeying Nebula flung herself

down on the roadway, her head against the rough surface. Lance looked down at her in wonder, trying to fathom what her intention was. He soon discovered. The hard road surface catching in the wadding about her eyes tore it free. She rolled over and glared up at him just as he stooped towards her. In that instant he met the full impact of her terrifying brain and it felt as though he had been hit with a sledgehammer. Just for an instant he saw her eyes blazing at him — red and venomous, then whatever mental wave it was that she hurled at him took effect. His legs buckled and he crashed into the ditch at the roadside.

He was as petrified in movement as Jeff had once been, but he was not completely knocked out. He heard Nebula in the grass as she came down towards him, evidently to finish off the job she had begun. He steeled himself for what he expected would be the final shattering vibration — but before it happened the wailing of a police siren grew loud on the morning air.

Nebula hesitated, the moaning coming

rapidly nearer. She gazed fixedly at half a dozen powerful police cars in the distance, sweeping onwards rapidly. Immediately she got on the move, leaving Lance where he lay, his face buried in the earth, his limbs powerless.

The cars swept by. Lance heard them go; but they did not seem to go very far. At least one of them returned. There was the slamming of car doors and crunch of feet on gravel — then he was seized and hauled up to the roadway. He lay gazing at grim faces regarding him.

'Lance Barclay!' one of the men exclaimed in surprise. 'I thought we saw a man's legs sticking out of the grass as we went by. How bad is it, sir?' he asked, peering at Lance closely.

He could not move even an eyelid, so the man straightened up again.

'Paralysis case — same as Mr. Walcott once got. We'd better rush him back to hospital. The rest of the boys had better look around here. Nebula, the Assistant Commissioner and the President may be about — Or at any rate the men will. God knows where that woman's gone.'

Lance strove frantically to break the steel grip on his nervous system. He wanted to tell the men to follow the Assistant Commissioner and the President; he wanted to tell them Nebula could not be far away. But all he could do was gaze fixedly at the morning sky and watch a lark go sailing into the sunlight. Then complete collapse came suddenly and the rest was darkness.

Since, when he came to himself, he found nervous control had returned he gathered that his case had exactly duplicated that of Jeff who, at an earlier date, had only just escaped with his life. The hospital surgeon confirmed the fact. As for convalescence, it was rapid, chiefly because of Lance's almost frantic desire to know what events were transpiring. He got the facts from the Head of the Intelligence Division of Scotland Yard, a hard-faced, unsentimental man by the name of Roper.

'Things aren't at all good, Mr. Barclay,' he said, scowling as he sat at Lance's bedside. 'It's over ten days since we picked you up and the devil of a lot's happened since then . . . Strikes, sabotage, international tension — everything that we thought had gone forever is back in treble force. Naturally that damned woman is back of it all.'

'Naturally,' Lance added. 'She told me she intended fomenting trouble everywhere — But what about the Assistant Commissioner and the President? Haven't you found them?'

'Neither them nor Nebula. We don't even know where to look, as far as the men are concerned.'

'You'll find them in Nebula's hideout amidst the Downs — or at least that was where we were heading when things happened. What I'm wondering is, how did you get on our tail?'

'Simple enough. We got information that the special car which had gone to the airport to pick you up had been waylaid and the driver wiped out. That meant some other car had been substituted, with presumably a driver in Nebula's employ. We drove to the airport, were told in which direction the phoney car had gone, and by enquiries learned it had taken the south coast road. So we followed; then we spotted you — or at any rate your legs — and you know the rest. We spent a good twelve hours searching in relays for Nebula and the other two men, but no luck. And if they're in Nebulas hideout we still won't have any luck. The place is impregnable. Several men in the past have tried to get into it and never been seen again.'

Lance sat musing, propped up in the bed. 'You know about poor Jeff Walcott, of course, from the radio message the President sent?'

'Yes. I know. Everybody does. Too bad: Jeff Walcott was a grand fellow. Incidentally, following on the death of Elsa Crane other notables have been mysteriously eliminated in the past ten days — Walter Lansford, our foremost space-rocket designer, for one; Calvin Thomas for another, the man who could have brought immense prosperity to England and the Americas by constructing the Atlantic tunnel. And Henry Mason is dead, too. He had charge of new city construction. This creature in the guise of a woman has taken care of everything with diabolical efficiency, and she must have hosts of agents working for her.'

'She has,' Lance muttered. 'Most of them obeying post-hypnotic orders. And you say she's stirring up the maximum of strife everywhere?'

'Everywhere.' Roper gave a gloomy nod. 'Industry is about at a standstill — not only here but in practically every civilised country, and when things are like that the people are about ready to revolt. Instead of that I'm afraid we're going to have war. Every nation seems to be shouting insults at every other nation.'

'Somehow,' Lance said, thinking, 'that lair of hers has got to be penetrated. It is there where she must have assembled all the scientific gadgets that make her so dangerous — the instruments which can produce such powerful hypnosis over big masses of people, the machine shops where she must be manufacturing equipment far ahead of ours. Even the airplane in which she flew to Africa must have been infinitely ahead of anything we've yet produced. By the way, what happened to it? Have our scientists been able to examine it?'

Roper shook his head. 'It was gone before we could get to it — removed by one or more of her agents.'

Lance shrugged. 'To be expected, I suppose . . . But in that hideout also there will be the President and the Assistant Commissioner. They must be rescued.'

'My guess is that they'll be dead by now,' Roper said, but Lance shook his head.

'I don't think so. Nebula is anxious to have the President and Assistant Commissioner witness her final triumph over the fools called Earth people. She's working out a scheme of vengeance for something which our ancestors did.'

'Oh?' Roper looked vague — so Lance gave him the facts insofar as he judged the Yard man would be able to understand them.

'And what did our ancestors do to make this woman such an enemy?' he asked, pondering.

'I don't know: I never got as far as finding out, but because I'm a scientist and because the facts may make scientific history I'm going to try and get the details somehow. All else apart, inspector, the asteroids have been a scientific puzzle to scientists since the earliest time. Something mighty big blew a planet to fragments — and Nebula is the only living creature who has the answer. So I've more reasons than one for trying to penetrate that hideout of hers.'

'But you don't suppose she'll tell you anything, do you?'

'Of her own accord, no — unless she gets into a communicative mood as she did before. My aim is to perhaps use one or other of the instruments she must possess to make her talk . . . And there is also another point. Twice she unwittingly gave away the fact that she can be destroyed, and that is by disintegration. In fact that was how she died in her much earlier life.'

'What's the difference between disintegration or a bullet? They both bring death, don't they?'

'To Nebula a bullet doesn't bring death: she can assimilate it as easily as you or I can assimilate the food we eat and take it into our bloodstream. But disintegration means to blow every atomic cluster away from every other atomic cluster: reduce a body to cosmic dust. If that happened to Nebula she would cease to exist for even she would not assimilate that. It happened to her before when her world was destroyed, and I could tell when she referred to it that it is the one thing she fears. If I could only get her between the opposing globes of the transmutation laboratory *I'd* make her talk, I'd make her sweat her heart out begging for mercy. Once caught between the energies of those globes she'd be shattered to millions of atomic parts which only chance could ever link up again.'

'As happened when she reappeared at the outset?'

'Exactly.'

Roper rubbed his chin. 'Well, if there's anything I can do to help you penetrate this hideout of hers I'll do it, of course. At the moment I'm in full charge of this Nebula business — and not enjoying one minute of it.'

'I don't think you can help me much, thanks all the same,' Lance responded. 'I'll have to act on my own. I'm the only one remaining on the outside of the fence, so to speak, and I'm the only one who's scientist enough to perhaps trap Nebula into making a false move . . . The moment I can get out of this infernal hospital I'll go to work on the job.'

'And rely on me for every facility,' Roper promised.

The only help Lance asked for, however, was to be driven to within a couple of miles of Nebula's suspected hideout. This was two days later, and even at that Lance had left hospital before time. But he felt he had to: he could not lie in bed thinking up schemes whilst the world was tumbling to bits round his ears.

He had timed it so that his arrival to within two miles of Nebula's hideout was in the early autumn evening. It was growing dark even as the police car started off on its return trip to London, leaving Lance in the midst of the Downs, their humped backs rising to the gloomy sky. Lost in the haze in the opposite direction was the sea. Lance did not make any moves. He settled down on the brown, dry grass and just waited — with a purpose. If, as was more than likely, he had been detected making his journey here somebody would come before long and deal with him. If nothing happened, then it could only mean that by some fluke he was not under observation. He did not delude himself into thinking that Nebula perhaps thought him dead. He remembered only too clearly that she had been just about to finish him off completely when the arrival of the police cars had frightened her away.

Darkness came. In the distance dim lights came up here and there — but not the usual bright brilliance since all power stations had ceased operating. This small but significant fact made Lance realise once again how far this alien being in the guise of an unforgettable woman had corroded the social fabric of the world.

Finally, as there seemed to be no sign of anything untoward happening, he began to move. Before making his trip he had completely memorised the scale maps at Scotland Yard — which showed the position of Nebula's hideout — the self-same 'factory' that had once been visited, therefore its location was exactly known. The job was going to be to enter it.

It took Lance an hour, making cautious progress in the mist that had come up from the sea, to reach the approximate location. The greyness was so enveloping he could not check on landmarks and make certain. Yet there did not seem to be anything unusual. Only the Downs, the faint signs of a moonrise appearing in the clearing sky above, and a suggestion of a breeze carrying the mist on its way. Then, in the intense silence, Lance heard something. Or rather he felt it. It was the buried vibration of something far beneath his feet. He smiled. There was a machine-room somewhere near here, deep down in the earth.

He began to explore the ground thoroughly, prepared to find some kind of artificial soil and grass that was hiding the underworld entrance. He was in the midst of his task when a faint whirring overhead like that of a monster bat attracted his attention. Crouching, he watched an airplane of peculiar design, without lights and making no noise with its motors, coming down out of the moonrise. It descended no more than a quarter of a mile away and immediately he got on the move towards it.

He was just in time to see it taxi-ing along the bumpy ground, still in silence, and the further it went the less visible it became. It was disappearing down some kind of ramp. At that Lance threw all caution to the winds and raced after it, speeding down an artificial slope in the wake of the plane and then pausing as behind him the entrance to the ramp closed like an eyelid. He was in total darkness, listening intently. The noise of buried industry was quite audible now, but for all the light there was he might as well have been in a tomb.

Then there was a metallic sound. He blinked and crouched as enormous metal doors slid aside on runners, the glare of a huge space beyond silhouetting the plane clearly. It was no longer on the move but a slender figure in slacks and a blouse had alighted from it and was heading into the blaze of light beyond. Lance knew that figure immediately and the arrogant angle of the head with its mass of hair. Evidently the plane was always left here, ready for instant use, whilst Nebula herself moved on into the busy regions beyond.

Lance had a few seconds in which to make up his mind. Once beyond those vast doors Nebula would have them closed again and he certainly would never be able to gain entrance — so once again he took a chance. He waited until the girl had passed beyond them and then watched for them to start closing. After a while they did so, moving ponderously towards each other. At the last second he hopped through the fast narrowing gap and reached the other side as the metal flanges locked with a ringing clangour. He found he was on a high, rocky ledge.

Still not quite able to believe his good fortune at having got within the 'lair' he threw himself on his face to avoid detection, and in this position surveyed the scene before him. There was no doubt but what he was in a type of factory, most of its floor space devoted to all manner of equipment. Some of it he could identify as electrical, but a big percentage of the stuff was right outside his comprehension. In the far distance he espied the gleaming spheres of a transmutation equipment and his eyes gleamed as a thought passed through his mind.

There seemed to be quite a few workers in the space, men and women — dressed in overalls and tending the machinery, though what purpose the machinery could serve Lance found hard to imagine.

He caught sight of Nebula again as he studied the scene. She was in the distance now, heading for a door — of which there were about a dozen let into the metallic wall. Lighting seemed to be produced by three globes, each of enormous size and emitting a blazing yet glareless effulgence which was way ahead of anything Lance had ever experienced before. In fact the formidable signs of scientific genius were profoundly disturbing. If ever a woman had the wherewithal to destroy a planet it was Nebula.

'Just what are you doing here, Lance? Investigating?'

Lance twisted his head in astonishment as the question came to him quite politely. He had just seen Nebula vanish through that distant doorway — yet now she stood right behind him in her slacks and grey blouse. There was no savagery in her expression and her eyes were deep amethyst pools instead of being red. In fact she was the original Nebula of the black hair and green skin.

Lance got up slowly and glanced back towards the distant doorway.

'Only a double,' Nebula explained, her smile mocking. 'I have three women who closely resemble me in stature — and they dress as I do. From their appearance at a distance one would say they *are* me. At close quarters the differences are obvious. And naturally they have not my intelligence.'

'I thought my arrival in here was too good to be true,' Lance said, shrugging.

'You thought correctly. My radio

operators, who also run detectors, knew exactly what you were up to. Every move you have made since leaving hospital has been perfectly plain. I was attending to business elsewhere when I was informed by radio that you were investigating — so I returned by 'plane. Still by radio I was informed the detectors said you were right behind me. I gave you every opportunity to come inside, ordered one of my doubles to confuse the issue, and I have been standing here watching you ever since you lay down on your face.'

Lance said nothing. He took his automatic from his pocket and held it steadily, his eyes fixed on the girl. She returned his look and shrugged slightly.

'If you fire that, Lance, two things will happen. I shall remain unhurt because bullets cannot affect me, and the noise of the gun will bring instant help. You would get the worst of the bargain.'

'I'll get that anyway, won't I?' he snapped.

'I'm not sure. After all, you are the only one left to witness my final victory.'

'The only one?' Lance's eyes sharpened. 'You mean you have disposed of the

President and Assistant Commissioner?'

'Certainly. My man in the car drove them here and, when I had finally managed to break free of that wire holding my wrists I followed on. I discovered that the President and Assistant Commissioner had been foolish enough to try and make a break for it — so, of course, they sealed their own fate.'

Lance lowered his automatic slowly, fully aware it was a useless weapon as far as dealing with Nebula was concerned.

'Since you have decided to spare me for the time being, so I can share your victory, why not tell me what all this equipment is for?'

'You cannot gain the mastery of a planet by agents alone, Lance,' Nebula responded. 'It demands scientific equipment. Some of it comprises hypnotic amplifiers; elsewhere spaceships are under construction because, once Earth is under my control, I shall, of course, spread my influence to other worlds. Space travel was an accepted science by the race to which I belonged. I intend to develop it still further — out to the stars.

'And then,' Nebula continued, turning to look at the wilderness of equipment, 'there is radio apparatus in various forms. Some of it is normal radio-television; in other cases it has X-ray qualities. In a less orthodox form I use it for the amplification of thought waves or the reading of minds over a distance . . . In fact everything in this retreat of mine is scientific to the nth degree. I am simply using the knowledge I possess, inherited from my race.'

'Which means that one might call this hideout of yours a couple of centuries ahead of the present time in the matter of scientific development.'

'At least that. I have men and women working for me — those whom I specially selected, and who will never give me away.'

'I shouldn't like to trust them that far if I were in your position,' Lance remarked.

'I have taken precautions, believe me. I have dealt with the brains of every one of them. If any of them were to leave here, which they won't, they would be unable to remember a thing. Their subconscious mind areas are completely blacked out. My agents have the same 'complaint'. They cannot give me away even if they wish, but they obey my order blindly. I find it quite interesting dealing with creatures so far below me in intellect.'

Lance did not respond. He surveyed the equipment, and the anode and cathode globes in the distance. The sight of them stirred him to another comment.

'I notice you have included transmutation amongst your accomplishments.'

'Of course. I require gold in considerable quantities to pay for the materials I need. I have made myself the wealthiest woman on the planet as well as the most powerful — yet nobody can touch me by legal or any other means because all the bank accounts I possess are in different names.'

'Your apparatus is recognisably similar to my own back at the Transmutation Laboratories — if somewhat more impressive,' Lance commented, musing. 'But I don't see any vacuum tube . . . '

'I *did* base it on your set-up,' Nebula admitted. 'I had plenty of opportunity to study it, remember. But I have incorporated many refinements of my own. I've dispensed with your clumsy vacuum tube, and instead employ an electromagnetic force field to contain the materials and energies involved.' She touched a control, and instantly the slightly raised dais between the mighty anode and cathode globes was surmounted by what looked like the top half of a giant soap bubble. It glittered with translucent colours.

Lance stared at it intently, then switched his gaze to the controls Nebula had activated, as she collapsed the field. 'Amazing! I'd like to see it in action sometime,' he said, striving to contain his eagerness. 'Do you have any transmutation work upcoming?'

'I do, as a matter of fact.' Nebula seemed pleased with Lance's flattery and interest. 'In order to boost the range and power of my thought-amplifier to encompass other countries, I shall need to coat the amplifier helmet with an amalgam of precious and rare metals, including transuranic elements. I shall need to create them with my apparatus. It is slow and exacting work, but in a few days I will be ready.'

'Other countries?' Lance was puzzled, and not a little fearful. 'What have you in mind?'

'So far, I have been able to foment trouble abroad by hypnotically manipulating key figures. But the next phase of my plan requires that I am able to control entire populations *en masse*. For that I require to modify my main thought amplifier helmet, to increase its range.' Nebula smiled cynically. 'Such is the joy of superior intelligence.'

'Conceit doesn't become you, Nebula. You're individual enough without that.'

She gave her gentle, deadly laugh. 'Not to be proud of one's accomplishments is false modesty, Lance. I am conceited, yes, because I have reason.'

'All the vices and not one virtue,' Lance said coldly, turning to look at her.

'I come from a race which had no virtue — and so do you. But something must have happened to you and your people of the later present-time because they actually have sentiment. Such a thing

168

did not exist in your ancestors.'

Lance felt he might be on the verge of learning the secret that still eluded him.

'You have said my ancestors destroyed your world. About what period did it happen in Earth history?'

'At the time of the Deluge . . . I think,' Nebula added, 'that you do not realise, when accusing me of ruthless cruelty, that your own race was, in the olden times, much worse than I could ever be.'

'I have no cause to realise it when you won't explain the facts.'

'Perhaps it cannot matter if I do,' Nebula said, musing. 'I suppose my victory will lose much of its point if you do not know my reason for wishing to wipe out the Earth people — or at least reduce them to slavery, to which end I am rapidly moving. Yes, I think I might show you the answer, where I would not to anybody else.'

'Thanks,' Lance growled. 'Though I'm surprised you pick on me for the favour. I suppose it's because you have no other worthwhile enemy left.'

'No, Lance. It's because I love you.'

Lance looked at her in incredulity. 'Because you love me! Great heavens, you don't even know the meaning of the emotion. You, who destroyed my wife and family — '

'Of course. For two reasons. I destroyed your children because, in adult life, they might provide more children for this detestable Earth race; and I destroyed your wife because as long as she lived you would love her. With her death I had the hope you might be swung towards me. Instead you turned into my bitterest enemy and, so far, the cleverest.'

'What else could you expect?'

'I misjudged the nature of an Earthman. I did not know he would take death so seriously. I never do, nor did any member of my race. But I haven't lost hope that one day I may claim you for my own. Though you have not my range of intelligence you have courage enough to fight me — and that is what I admire in you.'

Lance was about to give vent to his real feelings, then he checked himself. There was no doubt from Nebula's expression and voice that she meant what she said. Queer, lethal creature though she was she evidently had the emotions of a woman somewhere at root. It was the one thing that might cloud her scientific judgment. Lance was thinking of the anode and cathode globes and the quickest way to destroy her when he had learned all he wanted. He could see no other justice for such a creature.

As for love: he could better imagine himself fascinated by a serpent.

Perhaps, in her present mood, she might unfold the scientific secrets of the ages, and walk into a trap at the same time. Then Lance suddenly remembered that she could read thoughts and he blanked out his meditations abruptly. But apparently the girl was not concentrating on his mind. She was looking out pensively upon the busy men and women in the space below.

'Maybe I could forget the misfortunes of my family life,' Lance said at length, and at that Nebula looked at him quickly. He felt that now she really was trying to read his mind, but he kept his thoughts indecisive.

'You will think differently of me when you see my reasons for hatred,' Nebula responded. 'Come with me, then after a meal you shall see for yourself.'

7

Cataclysm

During the refreshment in Nebula's perfectly appointed private room Lance made a special point of dropping his hostile attitude and instead did all he could to appear friendly. And he found it a good notion. The girl was obviously in earnest regarding her affection for him and, had he not been constantly pervaded with memories of the things she had done — and would yet do — Lance could even have found her appeal irresistible. As it was he skated round the edge and made up his mind to watch for the supreme chance to destroy her.

When the meal was over she led the way into an ante room where there stood several scientific instruments of a radio design, two bakelite chairs screwed to the floor and, secured to the top of their high backs, two hemispheres studded with what looked like jewels and connected to a switchboard. Lance was unpleasantly reminded of an electric chair — or rather two chairs.

'Thought reading equipment,' Nebula explained, as he glanced at her. 'I sit in one chair and the person whose thoughts I wish to read sits in the other. The helmets are magnetic, and pick up the vibrations from the brain — not necessarily conscious thoughts but those memories buried deep under accruement of brain cells. In this instance you will read my brain. Into your mind will come a picture of events, which, to you, are but hazy history. You will have the feeling of being an independent observer.'

Lance nodded but did not say anything. He was conscious of a thrill at having at last got the chance to learn the secrets which had baffled his own scientific age and which the girl herself had held back so tenaciously.

He settled himself in the chair to which Nebula motioned, then she herself went to the switchboard and set the automatic controls. Returning to the twin chair she settled in it but said no word. Lance waited, the 'jewels' on the hemisphere over his head glowing brightly. Just for a moment he wondered if the girl had planned some novel way of killing him — and then he decided against it. To kill him was not her objective — at the moment.

Thus far he had got in his speculations when he felt as though he were reeling into space. It was a ghastly sensation like falling headlong down a shaft into bottomless nothing. Everything was totally dark, all outlines of the laboratory having vanished. Just as he thought he could bear no more of the hideous dropping — and yet felt utterly powerless to cry out — the darkness vanished and his brain steadied. He was not conscious of his body. He had only the conception of being an omnipotent eye surveying a most extraordinary scene.

He was looking upon a majestic city from what seemed to be a high ledge. The city was entirely lighted by a shadowless glow from somewhere within its mass. It was a city of graceful buildings — all apparently white metal or stone — orderly streets, and broad park-like spaces. The sky above it was nearly black, powdered with stars. One star gleamed more brilliantly than the rest, but was so distant it could hardly be called a sun.

'You are looking at the world of Nimatus,' came Nebula's disembodied voice. 'The city too is named Nimatus and is the only city on the planet. You are looking on something that existed aeons ago, which my memory of it has revived for you with photographic clearness. You behold the sun as seen from Nimatus. The nearest planetary neighbours are Mars and Jupiter. That is the planet which, through the agency of your ancestors, was blown to pieces and became the asteroids of today . . . At that time Nimatus a world of oxy-nitrogen atmosphere, fair internal heat, and generally satisfactory conditions. The distance from the sun made daylight negligible, so artificial light — which you see — was employed. Nimatus was the only city on the planet, but within it lay scientific power of the nth degree.'

Into Lance's mind flashed a series of

montaged impressions of giant machine rooms and laboratories stacked with all manner of scientific instruments; then the view changed to four highly intelligent-looking men studying an enormous wall-sized screen. Upon the screen was the image of yet another city, built entirely of vast buildings of stone. It was the embodiment of power yet did not seem, to Lance anyway, to have quite the same suggestion of scientific magnificence as Nimatus.

'That,' came Nebula's voice again, 'is the ruling city of Earth. In the dim distance you will behold the Sphinx and Pyramids, much later remembered forms of which still survive in your present age. That city was one of several in the Eastern regions of Earth. The rest of the planet was unpopulated at that time. There is no desert at this period: that came later when the stones of this mighty city were eroded through wind and wave.'

Once again came the series of brief glimpses, all seen through the huge telescopic mirror, of Earth's major stone city. It was thickly populated with people, all of them obviously of Eastern origin. Science abounded and there was a high social order, but it had not the finesse of Nimatus.

'That Earth race was a genuine one,' Nebula said. 'By which I mean that they were born on Earth in the first place and evolved from primitive man to the state of culture you see there. That covered a period of time from the Carboniferous Period to the time of what you call the Deluge.'

The telescopic mirror view changed to a group of Earthmen in solemn conclave. No words were audible, so again Nebula explained the situation.

'That is the ruling clique of the city, lords of Earth. They know that the presence of an alien runaway planet in the Solar System, rapidly heading sunwards because of his major gravity, is going to cause tremendous upheavals on Earth before long owing to changes in balance. The same upheavals will affect all the inner planets, but the outer ones will escape with nothing less than a shaking. What are Earth people to do to escape this oncoming disaster?'

The telescopic mirror shifted and revealed, for a brief while, the alien runaway planet hurtling through the void at thousands of miles an hour. A rare cosmic accident was in the process of taking place.

'Earth people hurriedly began an examination of neighbour planets,' Nebula continued. 'The inner worlds were useless, but the outer ones would be more or less safe. They decided on the nearest — Nimatus. Observe . . . '

The vision in Lance's brain was that of Earth scientists studying Nimatus through their telescopic equipment.

'The Earth people knew Nimatus was populated by a thriving race. They also knew that that race might be obliterated if they, the Earth people, invaded Nimatus with their engines of destruction. We of Nimatus were peaceful at that time and had few defensive weapons. Observe what happened . . . '

Earth and Nimatus both became visible in space, as if seen by an omniscient observer. From Earth there was hurtling a continuous stream of projectiles, each one of them arriving on Nimatus and exploding in a transient flash of flame. When Nebula's voice spoke again it was trembling with passion.

'What chance did *we* stand?' she demanded. 'We were a peaceful, scientific race, possessing — by normal standards — life eternal. Before we realized what was happening we found a bombardment of atomic projectiles raining upon us with ever-increasing fury. The Earth people were determined to destroy all life on Nimatus so as to make the planet safe for themselves to visit. Our city was destroyed. The very landscape began to become cratered. We lived through a hell of whelming destruction — but in the end *this* happened . . . '

Lance watched intently with his mind's eye and after a moment or two he beheld Nimatus exploding into a myriad fragments, flame belching, from its internal seams. Then, very gradually, the pieces began to drift towards each other and string themselves out in a long line of rocks and twisted metal. The birth of the asteroids had begun.

'The atomic bombs themselves did not cause that disaster,' Nebula explained, 'but they touched off a deep inner seam of highly explosive gas within our world. It lay close to the planet's core and possessed the explosive violence of hydrogen when ignited. The result was inevitable. The shell of our world already weakened by atomic attack, it simply split asunder under the explosion. We were flung into space, disintegrated by the unimaginable violence of the cataclysm . . . As for Earthlings, they had destroyed our world and its people and gained nothing. They had no alternative but to try and get into space before disaster struck their world. They might find another planet beyond shattered Nimatus to which they could migrate . . . '

Nebula paused, the mental vision still that of Earth and the clustered asteroids.

'But there was not time,' the girl resumed, her voice quivering. 'The destruction of their intended destination upset the Earth people's plans completely. Before they could make fresh plans or fly off into space the passing planet brought the maximum of destruction upon them. Though I did not visually see what happened I can reconstruct it from memory and records. Watch . . . '

Lance could do little else. Spellbound, he surveyed a reeling Earth from an apparent million miles distance in space. He saw the runaway planet passing through the inner system and heading for the sun, chained by his gravity. But in his whirlwind passage his mass produced disastrous effects on Mars and Earth. On Mars the air and oceans were whipped voidwards in the wake of the flying planet, stripping Mars bare and leaving him with arid sea bottoms and an atmosphere too thin to support life.

On Earth's moon craters began to appear as rock was torn out of its surface and shallow seas were blasted out of existence. Again the atmosphere was snatched away leaving a world naked lo the void.

On Earth itself landscapes shifted and changed position. The atmosphere envelope itself remained in place, chiefly because Earth's mass had a stronger hold than either that of Mars or the Moon. But below the atmosphere chaos reigned. Oceans rolled, mountain ranges changed places, vast deluges swamped down on the tortured landscape. The city of the scientists vanished under a mighty tidal wave, yet as the disturbance died down the seabed came up again and the oceans parted to left and right. The city had gone, buried forever under the still saturated sands of the former ocean bed.

'There were survivors,' came the voice of Nebula. 'But the hell they had endured had blasted from them all traces of reason and knowledge. They became savages and climbed the long, hard trail of evolution once again to the present day . . . '

Lance became slowly aware of the laboratory again, of the fact that he had a body and that Nebula was in the chair beside him. She got up after a moment and went to the switchboard, cutting out the power.

'Now you know,' she said. 'You — and every being on Earth — are a descendant of those original scientists. Therefore you also know why I hate you so, why I am resolved to pay back to Earthlings the wrong they did my race and world.'

Lance was silent. The scenes he had witnessed had left an indelible impression upon him. So much that he had known as scientific theory had now been proven.

'I am the avenger of my vanished people,' Nebula said, looking at him fixedly. 'We all had the gift of nervous control which makes adaptation a simple thing. I have used that gift to the full since I was re-created. By the law of chance my atoms, disintegrated in the cosmos, must have been drawn by the gravity of Earth and came towards it. Again by chance they were reformed into my former pattern because they happened to be in that vacuum tube when you infused it with atomic bombardment. I, of all the thousands who once lived on Nimatus, came back. I set out on my plan of vengeance . . . and I shall finish it!'

'In my belief,' Lance said at last, 'you have completely missed the point.'

'*Missed* it! I just don't understand!'

'I mean that had you used your recreation in an effort to exchange your scientific gifts for our hospitality we could have done so much. Instead you set out on a campaign of murder, domination, and death. Doesn't it occur to you that Earth people paid the price for their villainy aeons ago? Wasn't it just retribution that the Deluge overtook them and smashed their civilisation to bits? Wasn't it enough that the survivors were poor, hunted beings, little better than beasts, who had to fight all the way back up the ladder to the present day? On Nimatus destruction was immediate — the struggle for Earthlings, blasted of all reason and frightened even of the lightning, was far, far harder.'

Nebula was silent, her fists clenched at her sides.

'You have made the mistake of putting present day people in the same class as their ancestors. That is all wrong — though maybe it bears out a Biblical passage — 'The sins of the fathers shall be visited on the children'.'

Nebula shook her night-black head slowly. 'The people of today, Lance, are not one whit better in nature than were their ancestors: they hardly could be since they have sprung from the same stock. Before I started to overwhelm them with my superior science they were looking for ways to start the same campaign of pillage and domination intended by their progenitors. At present their activities have been confined to attacking neighbouring countries and fighting amongst themselves, but in future centuries they would have found a way to carry their aggression out into space to other worlds. But if anybody is to conquer other worlds it will be me. In the struggle between worlds, as between peoples and nations, victory goes to the most powerful. It is my absolute conviction that I was recreated for the sole purpose of destroying or mastering the race which obliterated my planet and race.'

'And nothing will alter that view?' Lance asked quietly.

'Nothing!'

He got up from the chair. 'That's a pity. For a while, as I beheld the reason for your vindictiveness, I could almost have forgiven you — have believed that you really do love me. But not any more.

Since you won't forsake your plan even though I have shown you where you fall into error, we remain as enemies, Nebula. I am an Earthman and staunch to my race. I shall fight for its liberation from you. Just as you, of another race, and world, are determined to fulfil your own destiny.'

For just a moment, as she gazed at Lance's stony features, Nebula looked as any other woman anywhere might look at discovering her love is unrequited. Her eyes flamed for a second or two and Lance had to keep an iron grip on himself to prevent his brain being overpowered; then Nebula relaxed again.

'Not that way,' she said, shaking her head. 'You shall see my complete domination before you die . . . At the moment,' she continued, changing the subject, 'I have every country on this planet paralysed, and my next move is going to be mass-hypnosis through my super amplifier to force the communities to do exactly as I say. I intend to make Earthlings work for me, knowing me only as some shadowy but all powerful being who cannot be denied.'

'In fact a world of robots, forced by hypnosis to blind obedience to your orders?' Lance said coldly. 'You mean to sacrifice the people of this world to one ideal — conquest of other worlds?'

'Certainly. I have immortality myself and because Earth is not big enough for my plans I must include other worlds. Earth people are only fit to be workers and slaves . . .'

Since he said nothing she added, 'You will be free to roam about this underground retreat of mine as you wish chiefly because there is nothing you can do to harm my activities. Then, when I have achieved my purpose — and you have seen it — I shall kill you.'

Since Lance still made no answer she turned impatiently to the door and snatched it open.

'Come with me,' she ordered. 'I will arrange a suite for you. Until your demise I will grant you the comforts of an honoured guest.'

Lance realised in the days which followed — days measured only on the

188

clocks in the buried retreat — how subtly female was Nebula's plan. As she had said, he had every comfort, a man to wait on him, a luxurious suite, and was allowed to wander as he chose through the scientific wilderness — yet he was as impotent to do anything to stop Nebula as an ant would be to stop a power house.

Much of the time she spent in the radio department issuing orders over secret wavebands to her agents; for the rest she spent it with the transmutation equipment, creating the rare metals she needed to boost the power of her overseas hypnosis amplifier.

Occasionally, through X-ray mirrors, Lance was forced to watch the mentally-chained myriads of Britain marching about their cities in accordance with the orders of the Mistress. All normal life had gone. Every big city, every town, village and hamlet had its people nailed down either by hypnosis or the relentless control of agents.

In time, gigantic foundries and machine-room plants grew up on wasteland as spaceship workshops were erected. With the precision of robots, overalled men and women, every one docketed and indexed, went to work on the task of preparing the greatest offensive armada ever seen on a planet. It was more than obvious to Lance that, having reached her objective of subjugating his own countrymen and women to her will, Nebula was placing no limits on her ambitions, and there seemed to be no way of stopping her achieving world domination, unless —

It was time for him to put his plan into operation.

8

Vengeance

From that moment he dropped his hostile attitude towards the girl and instead sought her favours. For a while it was obvious she distrusted him, but being unable to read anything ulterior from his thoughts, which he deliberately kept blank, she finally began to believe his protestations.

'You tell me now that you do love me,' she said, when he had sought an audience with her in her private suite. 'You have told me that many times. Why do you change so? When I last had a talk with you of any length you swore to be my everlasting enemy.'

'I know. Because I thought then you could not carry out your scheme of vengeance and because I also thought I might be able to destroy you . . . Now I know differently. And I have had time to think. You have granted me liberty and comfort even though I did swear I was your enemy. I begin to think I have been a fool. You are cleverer than I, Nebula, and I must admit it.'

She waited, her enormous amethyst eyes fixed upon him, her beautiful face half hopeful. It was the look of a woman and not a scientific monster.

'I *do* love you,' Lance finished quietly. 'As an Earthman, and knowing the things you have done to my race and family, I have fought against confessing the fact — but it's too strong for me. Whatever you want me to do I will do — willingly. I am prepared to be your slave, and you won't need to use hypnosis, either.'

Nebula considered. 'I wish I could believe you,' she said at last, 'but I feel suspicious of your change of mood — and I am even more suspicious when I cannot read your inner thoughts. On the other hand you may mean what you say. Speaking as a woman, Lance, I still want you for my own, as I told you at first — but I have to be sure. Work beside me and let me see how loyal your are.'

'That's all I ask,' Lance responded eagerly.

'Very well. I am on the verge of completing my creation of the metals I need for my overseas thought amplifier helmet. You can assist. Come with me!'

Lance followed the girl to a room adjoining that holding the thought reading equipment. On a workbench therein reposed a golden helmet, not unlike the helmet Lance had already used in that it was covered with strange jewel-like protrusions, but it was considerably larger, and narrowed at its base, ending in an odd cage-like arrangement of metal tubing.

'I take it that caging at the bottom is to support the weight of the helmet when it rests on your shoulders?' Lance asked, studying it.

'Yes, it is quite heavy — and will be heavier still when I add its final coating. I want you to carry it for me to the transmutation room — and on no account drop it! It is extremely delicate!' The girl gave him a malignant warning glance as he picked it up in both hands.

'Don't worry. I shan't drop it.' Lance forced a smile as he deliberately blanked his thoughts so that Nebula could not pick up any hint of the idea that had suddenly flared into his mind like a nova.

He followed the girl out of the room, and at length they were crossing the scientific expanse towards the transmutation globes.

Nebula crossed to a metal workbench near to the main switchboard. On it was a mass of apparatus and instruments, which, to Lance, were inexplicable, though he thought he recognized portable welding equipment. And to one side was a metal tray containing thin ingots of the metals Nebula had already created.

Nebula cleared a space in the middle. 'Put the helmet down here — carefully!' she instructed. 'I want to work on it as soon as I have created the final metals I need.

'You can't help me on the actual transmutations Lance,' Nebula stated. She indicated the massive switchboard. 'All of the dials and displays are of course in my own language, and in any case you have no idea of the special metal I am creating. However, you *can* handle the protective electromagnetic bubble, simply by switching it on and off to my direction. I'll show you which control switches to operate.'

Lance watched intently as the girl demonstrated for him. 'What about a vacuum?' he questioned. 'You can't operate without one because the very molecules of the air would contaminate your materials. That's why I used a vacuum tube — '

'That's all taken care of,' Nebula smiled contemptuously. 'Once the force field is established, all the gases inside it are drawn off magnetically and expelled through the field itself, which then seals itself when the last gas molecule is expelled. Here is the switch which activates it . . . '

For the next hour Lance watched — through tinted goggles the girl had provided for both of them — the fearsome energy coils flashing between the mighty globes. The workshop was lighted intermittently by blinding glares and intense shadows, and Lance was not slow to notice that it caused the other men and women technicians to keep a considerable distance away from them, where they concerned themselves with their own particular tasks. For the moment, he and Nebula were effectively alone. That was something he had been counting on.

Three times, Lance collapsed and recreated the field as Nebula directed. The artificial lightning flickered through all the colours of the spectrum, flashing down the massive earthing columns into the floor, as the bombardment of energy transformed one element or isotope into another, by increasing or decreasing the number of electrons and protons in their nuclei. At last Nebula cut the power, and removed her goggles. The sudden silence was distinctly eerie. For a minute or two she studied the readings on the switch-board, then she straightened, evidently satisfied. 'Switch off the field!' she instructed sharply. 'The metal is now perfect, and is ready for collection.'

'Then it isn't radioactive?' Lance

questioned. 'Even though you've been dealing with transuranic elements?'

Nebula gave her superior smile. 'With my mastery of atomic processes, that trifling detail has been overcome.' Then her voice sharpened as she added: 'Go and collect the metal and bring it over to the bench.'

Lance gave a start, as something like an electric shock flashed through his mind. *Nebula was still wary of him!* She evidently had no intention of setting foot on the operating dais between the mighty globes herself, and thus putting herself in the firing line of the destructive energies!

But Lance himself had already anticipated this, and so did not hesitate for even a split second. *Had* he done so, then Nebula's suspicions would have been aroused, and his own fate would have been sealed. As it was he rose smoothly from his seat, tossing his own goggles aside. 'Of course!' he said, moving forward. Out of the corner of his eye he saw that Nebula had remained seated, evidently re-checking her readings.

But instead of making for the dais,

Lance suddenly darted to one side. Before Nebula could grasp what was happening, he had snatched up the golden globe of the thought amplifier. He twirled to face her, raising it above his head.

Instantly Nebula was on her feet, running towards him, her face a mask of malevolent fury.

'*Lance!*' she screamed. '*You fool!* What are you doing? Give me that amplifier —!'

As she advanced towards him, hands outstretched, Lance could see her eyes beginning to change. They flashed through a bewildering change of colours, and began to settle to a dangerous red. Realising he was within seconds of death, Lance acted.

'You want it, Nebula? Here — *catch*!'

To the girl's baffled fury, he flung the heavy globe high over her head. She twirled helplessly, watching it sail through the air, then crash down — right in the centre of the dais, actually striking the small pile of metal, and bouncing off it with a loud clang, before spinning to rest on the far side of the dais.

'*You idiot!*' Nebula screamed, instinctively running after it and jumping onto

the dais. 'If that amplifier is *damaged* — !'
She threw herself to her knees, snatching
at the fallen globe.

Lance, too, had been moving quickly
— straight for the switchboard!

Diving forward, he slammed in the
switch that activated the electromagnetic
force field. Instantly a hemisphere of force
surrounded Nebula as she scrambled to
her feet, clutching the globe.

Her features contorted with fury as she
realized how she had been tricked into
mounting the dais. Then just as quickly
she seemed to regain her composure. She
laid the helmet carefully back down on
the dais, and walked towards Lance. He
watched her narrowly from where he sat
at the switchboard, breathing hard, and
perspiration trickling down his face.

Nebula pulled up short near the edge
of the dais as she encountered the edge of
the force field. She was clearly visible, as
if seen through thick glass.

'Lance! Lance! What do you think you're
doing?' Her voice was oddly muffled, but
still audible for a short distance. 'Collapse
the field — let me out of here!'

He took no notice, and glanced around him. He smiled grimly as he saw that nobody was moving towards them. Most of them were in a deeply hypnotic state anyway, concentrating on their particular tasks, and those that weren't were still unaware that anything was amiss. He turned as Nebula continued haranguing him, her muffled words reaching him clearly enough.

'You can't get away with this! Even if they can't hear me, my agents will soon see me. They'll shoot you dead before releasing me! Let me out of here now, and I'll spare your life — '

Lance gave a mirthless smile. 'That's just what I don't intend to do, Nebula. I've worked a long time for this moment, and now I'm going to make full use of it.'

'If you think you can kill me by withdrawing the air from inside here, you're vastly mistaken!' Lance saw that her composure was beginning to slip, her face becoming hideous in its rage. 'I can survive in a vacuum for long enough for rescue to come — '

'Possibly you might,' Lance interrupted.

'But that isn't going to save you from what I have in mind: there isn't going to be enough of you left *to* survive! I've planned this thoroughly, Nebula, as I vowed to do from the moment I saw that you didn't intend to mend your ways. What I am about to do now may be considered as justice. Justice for the millions you've killed, enslaved, or smashed down with your superior intelligence and inhuman nature. You are going to *die* here, long before any help can reach you.'

Nebula's expression changed a little. The hardness went out of it. The palms of her hands were pressed against the edge of the force field and entreaty came into her fathomless eyes.

'Lance! Lance, listen to me! You wouldn't kill me! We battle with each other, yes, because we each have strong individuality — but we respect each other at heart!'

'My respect for you died when you refused to see that modern Earthlings are not responsible for what their ancestors did.'

'You can't kill me!' she shouted,

banging her fists on the invisible barrier. 'You can't! I'm immortal! You've forgotten that!'

'You are immortal except when disintegration utterly destroys all your atomic make-up. That happened on your world of Nimatus, and but for the Law of Chance you would have stayed dead for ever and Earth would have been spared your diabolical ministrations. You can adapt yourself to anything you say. Can you adapt yourself to the twenty million volts of the transmutation beams?'

'What — what are you talking about? You cannot read my switchboard — you cannot operate it, outside of the force field!' Nebula's voice was faltering. There were chinks in her armour and Lance drove home his thrusts without mercy.

'You forget that I have been watching you operate this apparatus, Nebula. Granted I have no idea how to *moderate* the beam, and how to add or subtract electrons to the metals being treated, but I *do* know how to switch it on — and to move it to maximum power!

'You will be disintegrated by massive

atomic bombardment. Not one atomic cluster will remain with another. It will be the end, Nebula — *the complete end!*'

'*Lance!*' she screamed hoarsely, tearing at the force field until blood began to show under her fingernails. 'You can't do it to me! You said you loved me!'

'I never loved you. You are alien and unspeakable. The whole Universe is jeopardised while you live. You killed my wife and children, and my best friend Jeff Walcott. That I have *never* forgiven . . . And as you die, Nebula, think of the secrets you have discovered which I shall claim in the name of Earth. You have given us every scientific discovery and enriched us by your unholy genius. All of that is ours, as recompense for the things you have done to us. Had you turned back on your road to conquest when I asked you I would never have worked to encompass your destruction — but now it has come to it nothing can turn me back.'

'Lance!' Nebula's voice was nearly sobbing with fear and remorse. 'Lance, I'll do anything you ask. I'll turn back. I'll make amends. I'll — '

'You can't,' he said curtly. 'You were born ruthless, and you'll die the same way.'

'I'll find a way to get back!' she screamed, her eyes blazing red, but harmless behind the translucent force screen. 'I'll come back! I'll come back, I tell you!'

He activated the switch to draw out the air so he could not hear her ravings and entreaties. Reaching out to the controls as he had seen Nebula do during the transmutations, he began to build up the power.

Suddenly, Nebula turned and bent down to pick up the thought amplifier helmet. She placed it over her head.

Lance gave a start. He had completely overlooked the apparatus. Whilst he had stopped Nebula from adapting it to extend its range overseas, it was still capable of operating locally — unless it was broken? He twisted round in his seat.

To his dismay, several men and women had broken off their tasks and were hurrying across the immense underground cavern towards him, answering

Nebula's telepathic summons. Most of them were carrying guns.

Without waiting any longer, Lance closed the switch that released the atomic bombardment. Fearsome energy coils flashed between the mighty globes. The nearest running figures halted momentarily as they were temporarily blinded by the glare. Lance slipped on his protective goggles, and began to slide a switch along its groove to the furthest notch. It moved slowly, and Lance cursed the fact that he had not had the time to build up the power to maximum before switching it on.

Inside the brightly glowing hemisphere Nebula seemed to burst into flames, and Lance beheld her glowing skeleton. For a brief second it seemed to him that the flesh was actually re-forming on her bones . . . then beneath his fingers the switch slid to its furthest notch.

Nebula's skeleton abruptly vanished in a coruscating explosion, became incandescent gas. The underground workshop seemed to rock and quiver as fireballs of twenty million volts crashed between the globes.

Lance closed the controlling switch. The dynamos whined to a standstill, the blinding streamers ceased. On the switchboard most of the displays died into black glass. He collapsed the force field, and immediately there was a small whooshing sound as the air rushed to fill the former vacuum on the dais.

Lance looked at the dais. It was completely empty. The metal, the helmet — and Nebula — had vanished. He experienced the familiar sensation of slight cramp and of having his hair lifted straight up by the static electricity. There was a reek of ozone. As he watched, a small cloud of tiny incandescent dust motes hung briefly in the air, and slowly began to disperse . . .

Lance drew his sleeve across his streaming face. He had done a ghastly job because he believed it had to be done. He looked about him. With Nebula's influence lifted from them, puzzled workers were beginning to gather nearby, holding their heads and rubbing their eyes, as if awakening from sleep.

Lance smiled. The hypnosis had been

lifted, and Nebula's machines would run themselves out. The authorities could take over these headquarters and straighten everything out. Everything Nebula had discovered was for Earthlings to use.

He looked again towards the empty dais. He had no regrets. The atomic fury had consumed not a woman but a scientific fiend, the most brilliant being the world had ever known. Wherever her brilliant mind had gone now it was disembodied and harmless to innocent millions.

As he turned away, a last tiny dust mote winked out of existence.

THE END

We do hope that you have enjoyed reading this large print book.

Did you know that all of our titles are available for purchase?

We publish a wide range of high quality large print books including:
Romances, Mysteries, Classics
General Fiction
Non Fiction and Westerns

Special interest titles available in large print are:
The Little Oxford Dictionary
Music Book, Song Book
Hymn Book, Service Book

Also available from us courtesy of Oxford University Press:
Young Readers' Dictionary
(large print edition)
Young Readers' Thesaurus
(large print edition)

For further information or a free brochure, please contact us at:
Ulverscroft Large Print Books Ltd.,
The Green, Bradgate Road, Anstey,
Leicester, LE7 7FU, England.
Tel: (00 44) **0116 236 4325**
Fax: (00 44) **0116 234 0205**